STRAWBERRY DONUTS AND SCANDAL

A DONUT TRUCK COZY MYSTERY

CINDY BELL

CONTENTS

Chapter 1	1
Chapter 2	17
Chapter 3	31
Chapter 4	43
Chapter 5	55
Chapter 6	69
Chapter 7	83
Chapter 8	99
Chapter 9	113
Chapter 10	129
Chapter 11	143
Chapter 12	157
Chapter 13	173
Chapter 14	187
Chapter 15	199
Also by Cindy Bell	213
About the Author	219
Baked Strawberry Donuts	221

Copyright © 2018 Cindy Bell

All rights reserved.

Cover Design by Annie Moril

All rights reserved. No part of this publication may be reproduced or transmitted in any form or by any means, electronic or mechanical, including photocopy, recording, or any information storage or retrieval system, without permission in writing from the publisher.

This is a work of fiction. The characters, incidents and locations portrayed in this book and the names herein are fictitious. Any similarity to or identification with the locations, names, characters or history of any person, product or entity is entirely coincidental and unintentional.

All trademarks and brands referred to in this book are for illustrative purposes only, are the property of their respective owners and not affiliated with this publication in any way. Any trademarks are being used without permission, and the publication of the trademark is not authorized by, associated with or sponsored by the trademark owner.

ISBN: 9781791624262

CHAPTER 1

The hiss and bubble of the fryer caused a smile to cross Brenda's lips. The *Donuts on the Move* truck had become like a second home for her. Its scents and furnishings were as familiar as her own kitchen, and the woman who stood across from her, her head bent to survey the crowd gathering beyond the open window of the truck, was as dear to her as her own family.

"It's getting crowded out there." Joyce glanced back over her shoulder as a smile creased her lips. "It's going to be quite a day."

"Yes, it is." Brenda turned her attention to the window as well. She caught sight of a shock of bright green hair and the unmistakable bounce in the step of a familiar, young woman. "Here comes Melissa. We're going to need her today."

"Guys!" Melissa's voice traveled up the steps before she did, enthusiastic as ever. "Alexa Vue is going to be here!"

"Alexa Vue?" Brenda raised an eyebrow as she watched the eighteen-year-old climb into the donut truck.

"Sure, you can't tell me that you haven't heard of her." She tugged a hairnet on over her short, green hair, then sighed. "She's one of the most famous food vloggers ever."

"Vlogger?" Joyce studied Melissa with some surprise. "What exactly is that?"

"Oh, a vlogger is kind of like a reporter, only instead of writing articles, she does videos, recording her thoughts, opinions, reviews, that kind of stuff. She then posts them on the internet." Melissa stepped up beside Brenda. "What can I do to help?"

"Pull these out in about forty seconds, I'm going to get another batch ready. We're going to need a lot of donuts today." Brenda wiped her hands on a towel and took a deep breath of the delicious smells in the truck. "I'm so glad we managed to get a spot at the food fair, and the possibility to be featured in the magazine."

"If Alexa Vue gives us a good review, we'll almost definitely get into the magazine." Melissa eyed the fryer.

"Alexa Vue," Brenda repeated the name and all of a sudden it sounded familiar to her. "Charlie mentioned her, I think. I think he's worked with her at the newspaper before. Though I doubt they did any projects together. I'm not sure how a financial and political reporter would work with a food vlogger."

"Interesting." Joyce grinned. "What did Charlie say about her?"

"As I recall he said she was talented, but quite full of herself." Brenda peered through the front window of the truck at the crowds gathering. Many were quite young, the same age or a bit older than Melissa. They'd hired Melissa to help with the truck when Brenda wasn't able to be there. Melissa had also babysat for her daughter a few times, so they were already familiar with each other. Since Joyce didn't bake, it was best to have another person who was able to take over things when Brenda wasn't available. Still in training, Melissa showed a lot of promise. Her baking instincts were far better than Brenda had expected.

"I imagine she is." Melissa laughed, then lifted the donuts out of the fryer. "But she deserves to be. She went from zero to famous in under two years. She's pretty amazing. Everyone tunes into her vlogs about new restaurants and old ones, too."

"Well, hopefully she likes donuts." Brenda frowned as she looked over the donuts that were ready to go into the fryer and oven. "I feel like maybe we should have come up with something more modern for this crowd. Are they going to be satisfied with regular old donuts?"

"There's nothing regular about our donuts." Joyce snapped her fingers. "Trust me, they're going to get snapped up, and if this Alexa character doesn't like them, then she's lost her mind."

"She'll love them." Melissa gave Brenda's shoulder a light pat. "Trust me. She's a sucker for sweets."

"I hope so." Brenda couldn't ignore the subtle flutter in her stomach. Anytime an opportunity presented itself for the truck to gain some attention, she found herself nervous and excited. When Joyce had first approached her with the crazy idea of running a donut truck together, she'd hesitated. She'd been a stay-at-home mother to her daughter since the day she was born, and she wasn't confident that she could handle helping Joyce run the business. However, with Joyce's financial investment and her steady support for her baking, as well as Charlie's eventual acceptance, *Donuts on the Move* was born. Now she couldn't imagine her life without it.

It took a lot of time and energy, but Brenda loved investing all of it. The only problem was, she felt pressured for it to be successful. Joyce sank a good portion of her savings into getting the truck and covering the first few months before it began to make a profit. She insisted all of the time that she was thrilled to have the truck, and their partnership, but Brenda still worried. She tended to worry, sometimes Charlie would call it her superpower. Sometimes he would roll his eyes, sigh, and give her a hug. That thought made her smile. The sound of a strong, gruff voice snapped her out of her thoughts.

"Hello, ladies." Detective Crackle's familiar face hovered in front of the window. "I thought I'd stop by to check on you."

"You mean to get a free donut?" Joyce smiled as she turned to face him.

"I would never turn down a donut, but I will be paying for it of course." His eyes sparkled as his lips curved into a mischievous smile.

"Coming right up." Brenda nodded and boxed up a few donuts for him. "What are you doing at an event like this?" She turned back to hand him the box and caught his eyes locked to Joyce's.

"He came here just to see us, Brenda." Joyce smiled and rested her elbows on the counter behind the window. "Isn't that right, Detective?"

"Well now, I did have a reason for being here. My boss asked me to check on the security that's been set up. He wants things to be sealed up tight." Detective Crackle took the box from Brenda. "Thanks so much, Brenda." He tossed the money on the counter.

"Thank you." Brenda got his change. She only charged him for one donut.

"Why is your boss so concerned about the security here?" Joyce straightened up again. "It's just a little food fair that the magazine is hosting."

"Apparently, there have been rumors about protestors showing up here. He wants to make sure that things don't get out of control." Detective Crackle shrugged, then turned his sharp eyes over the people that still poured into the area. "It's going to be quite a crowd, I can understand his concern."

"With you around, we shouldn't have anything to worry about." Brenda began to glaze some of the cooler donuts. "Should we try some different colors? What do you think, Melissa?"

"Go for some pink. That's Alexa's favorite color. She also loves strawberries." Melissa turned her attention to Detective Crackle. "I know she was involved in a few protests, maybe that's where the rumors are coming from. I haven't heard anything specific about it."

"That may be it." Detective Crackle nodded, then looked back through the window. "If any of you need anything just give me a call." He glanced at Brenda, nodded to Melissa, then gazed at Joyce for a lingering moment. "Anything at all."

"Thanks, Detective." Joyce headed towards the counter that they used as a small office space in the back section of the truck. "I'm sure we'll be fine!"

Brenda sighed as Joyce's dismissive tone rippled through the truck. Joyce and Detective Crackle's oil and water relationship made for some tense moments. She turned to apologize to the detective. Instead of his weathered face she was greeted by bright blue eyes and a smile painted in black lipstick. She wore black cuff bracelets covered in spikes, and a lacy, black top that revealed ivory skin. Her bright red hair was perched on the top of her head in a messy bun. Next to her stood a young man.

"Hi, is this donut truck organic and chemical free?" The woman blinked, then her smile spread even further to reveal dimples in her cheeks.

"We don't have any chemicals on the truck, if that's what you mean." Brenda tilted her head to the side as she tried to decide whether the young woman's hair was dyed or natural. The shade of red fascinated her as it sparkled in the sunlight. She presumed it must have been dyed.

"No, I mean, do you support the right to having clean and unadulterated food?" She frowned as she looked over the menu. "I don't see anything about what charities you contribute to."

"Oh actually, we mostly contribute to the local food pantries." Brenda cleared her throat, uncertain how to answer the questions. Most customers just wanted their donuts, they didn't really want to know much about the business itself. The inquisitive, young woman waited, as if she expected to hear more.

"It's not an organic truck, but everything is homemade." Melissa stepped up to the window and smiled. "Would you like to try a sample?"

"No, I only eat organic." She shook her head and walked off. The young man rolled his eyes and walked after her.

"That was strange, wasn't it?" Brenda glanced at Melissa.

"Not for this crowd. Young activists are huge fans of this particular magazine, *Restaurants Revealed*, mostly because it gives so much information about the restaurants, food businesses and foods that it features." Melissa grabbed one of the misshaped donuts that couldn't be sold, and took a bite. "She doesn't know what she's missing out on."

"Speaking of which—" Joyce tipped her head towards the window as she stepped away from the counter at the back of the truck.

Brenda turned back to find a long line of people. Once she had served them, she turned to Melissa.

"Do you think these protestors will cause a lot of trouble?"

"If you consider waving signs and shouting slogans trouble, maybe." Melissa flashed her a grin as she wiped down the counter. "I'm just kidding. Honestly, I don't know. Most of the time the protests are pretty peaceful, but it depends on the situation, too. With so many people attending today, and the tension over which businesses will get added to the magazine, I suppose anything could happen."

"You said Alexa was involved in protests of some kind?" Brenda began to make another batch of donuts. As she kneaded through the sticky dough she began to relax. Baking helped her journey to some of her favorite memories, which gave her a deep sense of peace.

"Yes, she staged a few protests against a farm that still uses pesticides on its produce. I mean, I think they all do in some form, but this particular farm uses one that is considered especially dangerous. It's a terrible thing, really. So many people have no idea what they are putting into their mouths and bodies." Melissa's eyes lingered on the swift movements of Brenda's hands. "You know it would be pretty easy to make some organic donuts, all we need to do is replace a few ingredients."

"No way. These are donuts. Just donuts, that's all. I like to keep things simple." Brenda brushed some flour across her hands to free some of the sticky dough.

"Brenda, we should listen to Melissa. She's more in touch with the youth around here. It doesn't hurt to cater to a new demographic." Joyce moved some glazed donuts to the display shelves, careful not to interfere with the detail of the decorative glaze.

"I guess you're right about that." Brenda laughed. "The only youth I'm in touch with is my six-year-old."

"I understand not wanting to overdo it. I can get a little excited about things." Melissa grabbed a piece of paper. "What if I just make a sign about how the truck is all homemade and supports local food suppliers?"

"All right, I guess that would be okay. But don't put anything about being vegan, because we use dairy products in the donuts. Plus, I don't want to do anything to take away from Vanessa's truck." Brenda winced as she looked across the truck at Joyce. "Remember when she went after the salad van?"

"Oh yes." Joyce held in her laughter. "She was quite irate."

"Okay, don't worry I'll be careful about what I say. You're not going to regret this, I'm sure it will get Alexa's attention. She doesn't strictly only eat organic food, so hopefully she'll try some donuts." Melissa set to work creating the sign.

Brenda sank her hands into some fresh dough and let her mind drift. Business began to pick up so much that Brenda had to skip making another batch of donuts and instead focus on the line of customers. Once Melissa added the sign to the outside of the truck, even more customers lined up at the truck. Surprised that it worked so well, Brenda turned around long enough to give Melissa a thumbs up, then turned back to find a phone pointed at her face. Behind the phone, stood a woman with bright pink streaks in her blonde hair. She began to speak even before Brenda could smile at her.

"I'm Alexa Vue, and I'm about to find out everything I can about *Donuts on the Move*. Who am I speaking with?" She lowered the phone enough to meet Brenda's eyes.

Brenda noticed that she wore spiked, black cuff bracelets as well. Though her eyes were brown, they seemed to shine with a hint of gold as they locked on to her.

"I'm Brenda," she stammered out her name. "My friend, Joyce and I run this truck."

"Oh, how sweet. I just love female owned businesses. So, tell me all about your product. How careful are you about what you put into your food?" Alexa aimed the phone directly at her again.

"Well, we make sure to use quality ingredients." Brenda cleared her throat, which felt as if it might grow too tight for her to take a breath.

"But are your ingredients organic and pure?" Alexa raised her eyebrows behind the phone.

"No, not organic, as for pure, well I'm not sure how to define that—"

"Never mind, can you please let our viewers know why they should take the time to eat at your truck?"

Brenda stared blankly into the back of the phone. She couldn't think of a single thing to say. As the seconds ticked by her heartbeat raced and she wondered if she would ever be able to speak again.

"It's okay, Brenda, you know everything about *Donuts on the Move*." Joyce's warm touch rubbed along the curve of Brenda's shoulder.

The moment she felt it, Brenda took a deep breath.

"Yes, of course. *Donuts on the Move* not only provides delicious fried and baked donuts, but it also guarantees friendly service and the option for custom donut requests." The more Brenda spoke about the business, the more relaxed and cheerful she became. By the time she finished, Alexa had lowered her phone.

"Okay, I think I have enough now." Alexa frowned as she skimmed her gaze over the donuts on display. "How can I be sure these are fresh?"

"They were just made, we put the time the batch came out above each display shelf." Brenda tipped her head towards the small signs over each shelf. "However, I have some just about to come out. If you would like one of those it will only take a few minutes to cool and frost them."

"That's all right, I'll just take two of those." Alexa pointed to two pink, strawberry donuts in the display case.

"Great choice." Brenda smiled and put the donuts in a bag. "On the house." She handed them to Alexa.

"Thanks." Alexa nodded as she pulled one out. She took a bite as she turned and walked away. Like Melissa had said, she obviously didn't insist on eating organic. Brenda noticed that a group of about ten people followed after Alexa. She hadn't even seen them standing there before.

"I don't think that went well." Brenda wiped the

sweat from her brow and began to breathe at a normal pace again.

"You did just fine, Brenda." Joyce slung her arm around her shoulders. "I'm sure she was quite impressed."

"I think so, too." Melissa stuck her head out through the front window of the truck as she watched the woman walk away. "By this time tomorrow, *Donuts on the Move* is going to be trending!"

"That's a good thing." Brenda patted her chest and took a deep breath. "I hope."

"It is." Melissa straightened up and grinned. "You're just going to have to make sure that you can keep up with all of the orders that you have. Good thing I'm around, huh?"

"Yes, it's a very good thing." Brenda smiled in return. "Speaking of which, we'd better get another batch going."

Brenda tried to find her peace with her hands in the dough, but instead her mind wandered to all of the mistakes she'd made on camera. By the time the next batch of donuts was ready, her stomach had twisted into knots.

"Melissa, do you think there's any way we could stop Alexa from publishing the vlog?" Hot water rushed over her hands as she washed them in the sink.

"Don't be silly, it'll be great." Melissa added more donuts to the display.

Brenda wanted to believe her, but she felt very nervous. She didn't think it would be great at all.

CHAPTER 2

Despite Brenda's apprehension about the interview, the day continued on, busier than she expected. Whenever there weren't customers waiting for donuts, Brenda gazed out through the front window at the increasing crowd. Despite the numerous people, she picked out Alexa easily. Perhaps the pink streaks made her stand out, but there were many people in the crowd with dyed hair. Something seemed to draw her attention to Alexa no matter where she was in the crowd. Perhaps it was because she never moved alone. When she moved, about five or six other people around her moved as well. She appeared to have a crew that floated around her like a strange cloud. Brenda didn't have too much time to look out the window, however, as the line at the donut truck continued to be constant throughout the day. They ran through their donuts quickly, and soon Brenda's mind was on how to keep up with the demand, rather than what Alexa might be up to.

"Melissa, here's a few more donuts we can put out, but this next batch needs to go on the racks or we're not going to have any donuts to sell." Brenda turned to her with a small tray.

"Great, let me get them up there." Melissa turned towards the window of the truck. "Uh oh, something's going on out there." She leaned across the counter to get a closer look at the disturbance in the crowd. "There's some kind of commotion."

"Commotion?" Joyce walked up next to her and tried to get a clear view as well. "Everyone seems to be gathering near the entrance. Brenda, you'd better take a look at this."

"What is it?" Brenda piled some donuts on a tray to cool, then lined up beside Joyce and Melissa. Right away she caught sight of the people gathering near the entrance of the town square. "Are they wearing gas masks?" Her heart began to pound. "What's going on here?"

"It's a protest against chemicals and pesticides in our food." Melissa frowned as she shook her head.

"It's meant to startle you, to make you think. But it doesn't seem like a wise thing to do in a crowd like this, people might panic."

"Just like Detective Crackle warned might happen." Brenda frowned as she took a step back. "He knew there might be a protest, and that it might get out of control. Maybe we should close up for the day." She began to gather what donuts remained on the display shelves.

"Wait, no we can't just shut down." Joyce continued to gaze out through the window. "Brenda, this is a special moment. Anytime people gather together to stand up for something they believe in, that's something that we should support."

"But it's causing all kinds of chaos." Brenda shook her head as she crossed her arms. "What if someone gets hurt?"

"Chaos can lead to some pretty great things." Joyce's soft palm rested on Brenda's back. "Let them have their say, because when it's a topic that matters to you, you will want to have your say as well."

"That's true." Brenda took a deep breath. "I guess I'm letting my cautious 'Mommy brain' rule."

"There's nothing wrong with that, but keep in mind there is one thing I know protesting does."

Joyce smiled as she glanced over at her friend. "It makes people hungry. We're going to want to stay open."

"Then I'd better get to making that next batch." Brenda shot a brief glance in the direction of the crowd, then returned to making the next batch of donuts. As she began to relax into the process, she nearly forgot about the protest.

When a sudden shout pierced through the noise of the crowd, Brenda jumped. She nearly dropped the donut she'd just glazed. "What was that?"

"Uh oh." Melissa hung out through the window, then reached for the lever that closed it. "We need to shut everything up real fast. Things are getting a little out of control."

"Here, let me get these out of the way." Joyce lunged for the display tray while Brenda collected the napkins and other items near the edge of the counter.

"What do you mean, out of control?" Brenda frowned as she looked out through the windshield of the truck. She could see the police surrounding the crowd of protesters. "Someone must have done something out of line."

"I bet Alexa had something to do with it. I saw her all alone near the front of the crowd just after the violence started and the police started closing in. I wonder if she did something to incite it?" Melissa narrowed her eyes. "She does like to stir things up."

"You're sure she was alone?" Brenda met her eyes.

"Yes. Why?" Melissa turned her attention to the crowd again.

"It just seems strange to me, because she had this group of people around her every time I saw her. Are you sure no one else was around her?" Brenda frowned as she saw the police break up the crowd and direct the protestors towards the parking lot.

"I'm sure. I noticed, because she was by herself. I thought about going over to say hello and talk to her about the interview. But we were so busy trying to catch up with the donuts that I didn't get the chance," Melissa said.

"Do you see her in the crowd, now?" Brenda did her best to get a good look at the crowd that had begun to surge towards the parking lot. Despite Alexa's unusual hair, she couldn't place the woman. Perhaps she had stirred the protestors up into a frenzy, and then bolted before she could face any consequences.

"No, I don't. But there is an officer heading this

way." Melissa tucked her hair back behind her ears. "You two do the talking, all right?"

"Melissa, are you okay?" Joyce caught her eye as she turned away and noticed she looked nervous.

"I'm fine, thanks, but I think they're coming to see you." Melissa headed farther back in the truck. "I'll start on these dishes."

Brenda started to question her further, but a sharp knock on the door of the truck drew her attention away. She popped it open to find one of the officers outside.

"Ma'am, we're asking everyone to close up for the day. It's the best way to make sure that things calm down." The officer glanced past her, into the truck and nodded to Joyce.

"Is everything okay out there?" Joyce frowned as she stepped up behind Brenda. "No one got hurt, I hope?"

"No, no one was hurt. But there were a few arguments, punches and some threats. We felt it was time to shut things down. We're going to stick around until we're sure that everyone has safely closed up and cleared the area. It's for everyone's safety." The officer shifted his stance a little closer to the door. "You don't have a problem with that, do you?"

STRAWBERRY DONUTS AND SCANDAL

"No, it's fine." Brenda forced a smile. "Thanks for your efforts, Officer. We'll get closed up as quickly as possible." She gave him a brief wave before she closed the door.

"You handled that well." Joyce stepped back farther into the truck. "I would have asked a lot more questions."

"Maybe I should have, but I didn't want to hold him up." Brenda looked past Joyce, to Melissa. The water in the sink was up to her elbows. "Melissa, you know you can talk to us about anything that might make you uncomfortable."

"It's nothing, really, I promise." She flashed them both a smile.

"We'd better get everything cleaned up." Joyce leaned closer to Brenda and spoke in a softer voice. "Let her be for now."

Brenda nodded, then began to box up the remaining donuts, while Joyce took care of the cash register. By the time they all left the truck, most of the town square and the surrounding area had cleared out.

"Not that long ago, this place was hopping, now it's like a ghost town." Brenda shook her head as she walked with Joyce and Melissa towards the parking lot. "It's strange how fast things can change."

"Yes, it is." Joyce gave her a brief hug, before she broke away to head towards her car. "See you tomorrow, ladies, bright and early!"

"I'll be here." Melissa waved to them both and jogged off to her car. She'd only recently gotten it, and though it was an older model, Brenda could see the excitement in the young woman's eyes every time she saw it. She could recall that special moment when she'd owned her first car. Yes, things certainly did change fast.

The subtle chirping of birds in the trees that lined Brenda's driveway gave her some sense of calm before she stepped out of the car. Brenda spent a few seconds any chance she could, just listening. Not for anything in particular, but to remind herself that a world existed beyond her thoughts and experiences. She'd spent most of the day making donuts, while the birds in the trees spent their morning just as busy she guessed, but for different reasons with different goals. Inside the house she knew her husband and daughter waited. She could imagine their day. He'd picked her up from school, and probably took her by the ice cream parlor as he always liked to do on Fridays, then spent the afternoon playing board games. It warmed her heart to know that her husband adored spending time with their daughter just as much as she did.

When Brenda stepped inside, she saw Sophie's book bag tossed near the front door, and her muddy sneakers piled up in the corner. She spotted her light jacket tossed over the back of a chair in the dining room, and a napkin from the ice cream parlor crumpled up on the middle of the table. She snatched it up as she walked past and smiled. Yes, they'd had a wonderful day.

"Where's my Sophie?" Brenda sang out her words as she walked through the dining room into the kitchen.

"Here we are." Sophie looked up from the board game on the kitchen table with a wide grin. "Mommy's home!"

"Thank goodness!" Charlie tossed down the dice in his hand. "Did you know that your daughter cheats?"

"What?" Brenda gasped and laughed at the same time as she slung her arms around her husband's neck. "That's not possible."

"I would never!" Sophie struggled to talk over her giggles.

Brenda let go of the strange events of the afternoon and settled in with her family for a wonderful night. Yes, there was a lot going on in the world, but this was her favorite place to be.

Brenda opened her eyes the next morning to the throb of a dull headache. She winced, turned her face into her pillow, and wished for just a moment that she didn't have to get out of bed. Then the reason why she needed to get out of bed surfaced in her mind. *Donuts on the Move*. No, she didn't always want to get up so early in the morning, but when she remembered why, her enthusiasm always returned. She slid out from under the covers as quietly as she could. Charlie's snores continued in their regular pattern. She knew that a little later he would wake up and cook breakfast for their daughter. He would read her jokes out of a joke book, and they would both laugh. It was their Saturday morning routine.

One good thing that came out of Brenda working in the donut truck was the time that Charlie and Sophie got to spend together. Since he worked from home a lot of the time, he was generally available for her, and their bond had increased quite a bit. Still, it always tugged at Brenda's heart to leave the house before her daughter was awake. For so many years she was Sophie's whole world, now they were discovering what it was like to be apart.

As Brenda headed out the door towards the car, she had to stifle a yawn. She wanted to arrive early so that there would be time to prepare extra donuts. She would often give Joyce a lift to the truck, but it was parked pretty much the same distance from both of their houses at the moment so there was no need.

After the large flow of customers the day before Brenda wanted to be more prepared. As she headed for the town square, she rolled down the window and took a deep breath of the moist pre-dawn air. She did find something magical about being awake when most people were asleep. As if she was part of some secret society that knew the thick quiet of the hour before the sun began to rise.

When Brenda pulled into the parking lot, she noticed a few other people were already there. Still a little bleary-eyed, she headed across the parking lot towards the truck. A loud screech of tires startled her just as she reached the other side. She spun on her heel as she expected to see an out-of-control car. Instead she saw something large hit the ground, and the dust that kicked up from the wildly spinning tires of the car that sped away.

The roar of the engine tore through the thick morning air like a jagged blade. She squinted as she took a few steps towards what had been left behind. Mentally, she became aware of what it was, long before she could psychologically accept what sprawled across the ground. A scream, not unlike the high-pitched sound of a few moments before, drew her out of her shocked state.

No, she wasn't mistaken. If she had been able to breathe, she might have screamed as well. Instead, she could only stare at the bright pink streaks that trailed through blonde hair, splayed across the ground. The unmoving figure drew the attention of the few people in the parking lot. A hand came into Brenda's line of vision as someone checked for a pulse. A fruitless endeavor, the hand disappeared, and a voice replaced it.

"She's dead, I'm pretty sure she's dead. Someone, call the police!"

The police. The words echoed through Brenda's mind. She could do better than that, she could call a detective.

Brenda's trembling grasp threatened to drop her phone as she pulled it out of her purse. She tightened her grip, and managed to select Detective Crackle's phone number. By the time the call connected, sirens sounded in the distance.

"Hello?" Detective Crackle's sleep-logged voice mumbled into her ear.

"Detective, it's Brenda, there's been an incident at the town square. Someone just left Alexa Vue's body in the middle of the parking lot. I thought you would want to know." She tensed as she noticed more cars entering the parking lot. "Someone, stop them from driving through here! Stop them!"

"Brenda, are you okay?" Detective Crackle's sharp tone cut through her panic.

"Yes, I just don't want them to drive over any evidence." She drew a few slow breaths in an attempt to control the panic that swelled within her. "Detective Crackle, are you going to come here?"

"Yes, I'll be there in just a few minutes. Stay safe, Brenda." He hung up the phone.

Jarred by his sudden absence, Brenda slid her phone back into her purse and took a quick survey of her surroundings. She noticed Vanessa from *Vanessa's Veggies*. From the way she trembled and hugged herself, Brenda guessed that the scream she heard came from her. Kevin from the burger truck stood over Alexa's body. He seemed to be shooing everyone back from the area. Good idea, she thought, as her head spun again. There were a few other familiar faces, but she couldn't put names to them at the moment. She also noticed a man she had never seen before. He stood out to her because his tall and broad body looked relaxed amongst the chaos. As the dawn began to break through the heavy morning clouds, the red and blue lights of approaching police cars splashed across the area in a myriad of colors.

Brenda's mind flashed back to the day before, when Alexa thrust the phone into her face and questioned her in ways that she didn't expect. The woman was so vibrant, so determined. Someone had cut all of that off. Every little sound in her surroundings seemed amplified as her senses sought to comprehend what she witnessed. How could this have happened?

CHAPTER 3

Numb from the shock of the event, Brenda managed to send a quick text to Joyce. She wanted to warn her about what had happened, to hopefully prevent her from experiencing the same shock when she turned up. However, her fingers trembled as she attempted to type, and the final message came out quite strange thanks to autocorrect. She sent another message in an attempt to make herself clearer. As she looked up from the phone, she caught sight of Detective Crackle walking towards her. The tension in his expression caused the lines in his weathered face to deepen. The morning sunlight did nothing to alleviate the dark circles that seemed to be perpetually present under his eyes.

"Brenda, are you okay?" He paused in front of her.

Brenda stared at him for a moment. She knew that the detective had spoken, but had yet to understand what the words meant. After a second passed, the sounds all around her slammed back into her mind, along with a wave of dizziness.

"I'm fine." She swallowed hard. "At least, I will be."

"All right." Detective Crackle placed one hand heavily on her shoulder and looked straight into her eyes. "Just take a deep breath. Count it out with me. One, two, three." His voice trailed off as he continued to hold her gaze.

Brenda followed his instructions, and realized that she might not have been breathing before he told her to. Of course logically she knew she was, but it sure didn't seem like it.

"Thanks." She brushed her hair back over her shoulders and took another deep breath. "I'm sorry, I just don't know what to make of all of this."

"You don't have to know right now." Detective Crackle pulled out a notepad and pen. "But if you don't mind, I'd like to pick your brain about what you saw, and heard. You are one of the few witnesses."

STRAWBERRY DONUTS AND SCANDAL

"Kevin, and Vanessa, they were both here." Brenda gestured to the others clustered together near the entrance of the town square.

"Yes, they were. Along with a few others. But I trust you the most, Brenda. I don't know them well. I know you will do your best to tell me what happened here." Detective Crackle tapped the pen lightly on the notepad. "Just tell me what you can remember."

"But I have no idea what happened here. That's what you're supposed to figure out." The muscles in her shoulders tensed as she tried to gain control of her emotions. "I mean is there really any explanation for something like this?"

"Not one that will ever satisfy the rational mind, but that doesn't mean we don't need to figure it out." Detective Crackle met her eyes again. "Brenda, tell me everything you can remember, it's very important."

"Right, sorry." She wiped at her eyes, then tried to focus. "The thing is I didn't even see much, Detective. I wish I had seen more, but I really didn't see anything at all."

"Just tell me what you can recall." He shifted from one foot to the other as his lips tensed.

"Okay, yes." After another breath Brenda

launched into a description of what she had seen. "I just remember turning around, and seeing Alexa on the ground." She stared towards the spot that was now roped off and surrounded by police. "But I only turned because I heard tires squeal. It was such a sudden sound. I turned around, and she was on the ground. The car was already almost out of the parking lot."

"You're sure? You didn't see anyone driving the car, or get into it?" He moved in front of her to regain her attention. "What exactly did you hear?"

"No, I didn't see the driver. I heard the tires, like I told you." Brenda frowned as she did her best to recall every bit of information she could.

"What about any passengers in the car? Could you tell if there was more than one person?" Detective Crackle scribbled on the notepad.

"I didn't notice. I mean, I don't think there was anyone else. But I can't be sure of that. I'm sorry." Brenda rubbed her hand across her forehead as her head started to spin again. "I told you what I saw, that was it. Then I tried to stop the other cars from coming into the lot. I thought maybe you'd be able to trace which tire tracks belonged to the car."

"That was a very smart move. Now, can you show me where the tire tracks are?" He turned towards the crime scene. "Maybe you could point them out to me?" He gestured to the dirty parking lot.

Brenda tried to look at the ground, but her eyes were drawn to the area where Alexa's body was. The area was surrounded by police, so she couldn't see anything, but she knew what was there. For a few seconds she stood in stunned silence.

"Brenda." His tone became firmer. "Brenda, I need you to try to work out which tire tracks belong to the car you saw."

"Uh, right." Brenda looked down at the ground. Her vision blurred as the multitude of tire tracks blurred together. "I think it was here, right here." She pointed to one deep groove, but there was another one not far from it. "Or maybe that one."

"Try to think back. You saw the car, Brenda. You saw it pull away, you know which direction it went in. It would be very helpful if you could narrow down which set of tire tracks it might be." Detective Crackle stepped up beside her and looked down at the ground as well. With the sun out in full force, her line of vision was clear. But she still had no idea which one to point to. At the time that she'd seen the car pull away, she hadn't really been paying attention to the car, but to the body left behind.

"I don't know." Brenda shoved her hands into her pockets. "I'm sorry, I just don't know."

"I'm sorry, Brenda, but you are my prime witness. Try and relax and see if you can remember anything. What kind of car was it? What color? What model?" He looked back at his pad. "I don't have anything here other than car, and squealing tires."

"I think it was gray, or silver, but it was still dark. I just don't know. I probably would have noticed if it was a brighter color. And it was a four door. I think. Yes, I'm sure it was a four door." Brenda's thoughts raced as she tried to summon back her memories of that moment. When it first happened, it seemed as if she would never be able to un-see it, but suddenly she wasn't confident in anything she recalled.

"Thanks Brenda. I know you've been through a lot, but now is the time when what you remember can make a big difference. What was the make? What was the model?"

"I don't know." Brenda shook her head. "I don't know much about cars. Okay?" She gulped out her words.

"Brenda!" Joyce ran the last few steps to her side. She shot Detective Crackle a harsh look.

"Can't you see that she's in shock?" She wrapped her arms around her.

"I know, but I need whatever information she might have." His gaze lingered on Joyce, then shifted back to Brenda. "Anything you can remember is helpful."

"I get that, but you want me to remember things I never saw. I just don't know what kind of car it was, I didn't see anyone. I had no idea that I needed to memorize as much as I could in those few seconds. I'm sorry." Brenda sighed, soothed by Joyce's presence. "I'm so glad that you're here."

"All right, I'll check in with you a little later." Detective Crackle adjusted his hat, looked between both women, then turned and walked away.

"He's such a buffoon." Joyce waved her hand through the air as she continued to hug her friend. "I don't know why you put up with him for so long."

"Joyce, he was just doing his job." Brenda sighed again, then wiped at her eyes. "It's not his fault I wasn't smart enough to remember anything that could help him catch the killer."

"Hey, none of that." Joyce frowned as she took a step back from her and met her eyes. "You didn't do anything wrong here. You did everything you could for Alexa."

"It all happened so fast." Brenda pressed her hand against her chest. "I still don't understand how it happened. How can someone just drive up and dump a body, then take off? All with no one stopping them? All with no one seeing anything of use?"

"No one expects to see something like that. The shock makes it hard for your brain to function as it normally would. It's too bad that the parking lot doesn't have any cameras." Joyce patted her hand. "Please don't be so hard on yourself."

"How can I not be?" Brenda frowned. "He's right. If I could only remember one helpful thing, maybe the killer would be found."

Joyce started to argue the point, but she was interrupted by a familiar voice.

"Hi Joyce, hi Brenda." Melissa walked up to them both, with her nose buried in her phone.

"Melissa, maybe you should go home." Brenda wrapped an arm around her shoulders as she steered her away from the crime scene. The wall of officers nearly blocked the view completely, but Brenda didn't want to risk her catching a glimpse of it. "Something terrible has happened."

"I already know." Melissa shifted out of Brenda's grasp enough to hold her phone out for both of them to see. "I can't believe it."

"You already know?" Joyce frowned as she stepped up closer.

"About Alexa's latest vlog, yes. Isn't that what you're talking about?" Melissa tapped the screen on her phone and a video began to play. "I saw it first thing this morning."

"She posted a vlog this morning?" Brenda leaned in closer for a clear view of the video.

Joyce stood on her toes and peered over Melissa's shoulder at the phone.

Alexa's image appeared on the screen. Instead of a friendly smile, her eyes stared heavily into the camera. As she spoke, her voice sounded breathless, her words fired off in rapid succession.

"I've made a terrible mistake. I can't apologize enough for it. I feel like the only way that I can make things right, is to come clean about this in the most public way I can. So please listen, and share this vlog with everyone you know. Authenticity is so important to me, as many of you know. I never would have gotten involved in this if I had known the whole story. But I can't be responsible for this any longer. I know I may lose a lot of my viewers over this, but I don't care." She took a deep breath. "Okay, the truth is—" Her words were cut off as the screen went black.

"Something has happened to her. Someone took her!" Melissa rewound the video a few seconds, then pointed out a shadow on the wall behind Alexa. "Someone came up behind her, see? Everyone is going crazy about it. You should see some of the comments people are making. Everything from it being a ghost, to it being her boyfriend. As far as I know she doesn't even have a boyfriend."

"I can see the shadow," Joyce whispered. "This really might be the moment that she was taken."

"I can't quite see it." Brenda narrowed her eyes as she stared at the frozen image on the screen. "But we should make sure Detective Crackle sees this."

"I can send him the link." Melissa looked up from the phone, her brows knitted as she noticed the officers and the police cars. "What's going on here? Is there something more I should know?"

"Oh Melissa, I know you were a fan of Alexa's." Brenda met the young woman's eyes. As intelligent and resourceful as Melissa could be, she was also still very young. "I'm sorry to tell you this, but Alexa was killed this morning. The police are trying to figure out what happened."

"What? Are you sure?" Melissa stumbled back a few steps. "But how could that be? This was just posted this morning."

"I'm sure." Brenda clasped her hands together and took a slow breath. "I saw her myself, Melissa. I'm very sorry."

"I knew something terrible had happened, I knew it. But this?" Melissa shook her head as she wrapped her arms around herself. "I never expected this. Who would do this to her?"

"That's what the police are going to find out." Brenda patted her shoulder and again steered her away from the crime scene. "And if there's anything we can do to help, we will. But as of right now, I think it would be best for all of us to just stay out of the way."

"Oh, there's Detective Crackle." Joyce glanced over at Melissa. "Can I borrow your phone, Melissa? I want to show him what you found."

"Sure, no problem." Melissa handed over her phone with a soft sniffle. "I hope he can figure out who did this."

"Me, too." Joyce accepted the phone, then gave Melissa's hand a light squeeze.

CHAPTER 4

As Joyce headed in the direction of Detective Crackle she noticed that he had Kevin cornered near his truck. The closer she came, the clearer the tension in the detective's muscles became. Kevin's cheeks flared a darker shade of red as she paused a few steps away from him and the detective.

"It's a simple question, Kevin, I would like to know where you were before you arrived here this morning." Detective Crackle squared his shoulders as he stared hard at Kevin.

"It's a question I don't have to answer. Unless you're ready to accuse me of something?" His thick hands balled into hard, red fists at his sides. "I won't stand here while you imply that I had something to do with Alexa's murder."

"I'm not implying anything. I'm simply asking you a question that you should be able to give me an answer to." Detective Crackle lifted his shoulders some as he leaned a bit closer to Kevin. "Perhaps it's you that's implying something by not answering the question."

"This is ridiculous. I had nothing to do with this. I'm not wasting anymore time here. If you want to ask me more questions, then you'd better go ahead and arrest me." Kevin's voice grew louder with every word he spoke, and seemed to punch through the noise of the officers and bystanders that had gathered.

"If that's what it takes to get some cooperation, then that just might be what I have to do." Detective Crackle rested one hand on the handcuffs that were attached to his belt. "Does it really need to come to that, Kevin, or do you think you can calm down?"

"I'll calm down when you leave me alone!" Kevin took a step towards the detective.

"Kevin!" Joyce stepped between them as Detective Crackle's hand went to the holster on his other hip. "Kevin, take a breath, it's all right." She patted the much larger man's chest and looked up into his eyes. They were spread so wide that she could see the whites of them beyond his dark lashes. "We all want the same thing here, don't we?"

"Joyce, careful." Detective Crackle grabbed her by the shoulder and drew her back a few steps.

"Yes, we all want the same thing." Kevin slid his hands into his pockets and lowered his eyes. "Like I said, Detective Crackle, if you need more information, you know what you have to do." He turned on his heel and walked away.

"What were you thinking?" Detective Crackle frowned as he released his grasp on Joyce, then stepped in front of her. "Why would you get in the middle of things like that?"

"Kevin just likes to run his mouth. He acts like a tough guy, but he's harmless." Joyce shook her head as she swept her gaze over his strained expression. "Why were you about to pull your gun on him?"

"He was threatening me. Someone has been murdered, Joyce. This isn't a game." Detective Crackle glanced over at the crowd gathered around the crime scene, then shifted his weighted gaze back to hers. "Please, be more careful."

"I could ask you to do the same. Picking a fight with someone twice your size isn't exactly a good idea." Joyce noticed a hint of concern flash through his eyes. She didn't see that often in the seasoned detective who always appeared to be in control. "Are you okay, Detective?"

"I will be." He sighed, reached up and pulled his hat from his head. "Once this murder is solved. Have you even considered that Alexa was here yesterday, as were you, as was Brenda, and myself?" Detective Crackle shoved his hat back on the top of his head. "It could have been either of you, but it just happened to be Alexa. My best guess is that whoever took her, spotted her here, yesterday, and enacted their plan sometime after that."

"I'm not so sure it was random." Joyce held out the cell phone to him. "I came to find you because Melissa, the new employee on the truck, saw this on Alexa's website this morning. I thought you should see it as soon as possible." She pressed play as he took the phone out of her hand. As he watched the video, she noticed the muscles in his face tighten as each moment passed. When he lowered the phone, his gaze was heavy.

"This may have been when she was abducted."

"Yes, I thought that, too." Joyce accepted the phone back from him. "Melissa and others who viewed the video spotted the shadow that came up behind Alexa just before the camera cut off."

"All right, I'm going to have the techs at the station dig into this. Thanks for bringing it to my attention." Detective Crackle pulled out his phone. His fingers moved swiftly across the keypad. Once he finished, he looked up at her again. "However, it doesn't excuse the risk you just took. Kevin could have hurt you. In future, please don't interrupt me when I'm questioning a suspect."

"I don't intend to. But I want you to answer one question." Joyce narrowed her eyes, studying every subtle nuance of his face as he nodded. "What if Kevin had taken a swing at you? What would you have done?"

The tension returned to his face. He cleared his throat, glanced over his shoulder, then looked back at her.

"Thanks again for your help with this. If you or Brenda hear anything more about it please let me know."

As Detective Crackle walked away, Joyce understood that his choice not to answer spoke volumes. She and her late husband Davey had discussions throughout his career in law enforcement, about when and why it was right to draw a gun on a suspect. They had rarely agreed on the topic. She guessed that if she and Detective

Crackle had the same discussion, they wouldn't agree either.

~

Brenda watched Joyce hurry away, then turned her attention back to Melissa.

"How are you holding up? I know that you are a fan of Alexa's work." She slipped her hand into hers. "This must be quite a shock for you."

"Yes, it is." Melissa sighed and wiped at her eyes. "I am a big fan. Lots of people are. I like that she's so honest. But I didn't like the review she did of the truck." She frowned as she glanced down at the ground. "I thought she would be more fair than that. It made me wonder if she's really so honest, or if she's just going for shock value most of the time."

"The vlog was bad, huh?" Brenda bit into the inside of her cheek to hide her gut reaction. Her cheeks still flushed with heat.

"There were some positive parts to it, but overall I thought she could have been a lot kinder." Melissa shook her head, her eyes narrowed. "I'm sorry, Brenda, I never should have encouraged you to do the vlog with her."

"It's all right. It's probably not that bad. Let's

take a look." She pulled out her phone and pulled up Alexa's website.

"Oh no, don't." Melissa tried to grab the phone from her hands. "Trust me, after what's happened today, it's nothing you need to see."

"It's all right. I want to see it. It's one of the last vlogs she recorded. Trust me, I won't get my feelings hurt." Brenda cleared her throat. She did tend to take things to heart. She'd give herself pep talks before walking into stressful situations, but the pep talks didn't always work. Still, she couldn't ignore the drive within her to see what Alexa had to say about her and the truck. It wasn't so much that she was curious about her opinion, it was more that she wanted to hear her voice again. She'd only met her briefly, and now faced with her death, she wanted to know everything she could about her.

"All right, but don't say that I didn't warn you."

"Warn you about what?" Joyce walked over to them, her hair out of place, and her eyes a bit wide.

"Joyce, are you okay?" Brenda looked up from her phone long enough to meet her friend's eyes. "Did something happen?"

"Nothing I couldn't handle." Joyce patted her hair back into place, then peered at the phone in Brenda's hand. "What are we watching?"

"Alexa's review of the truck." Brenda winced as she pressed the play button. "Apparently, it's not too good."

"Let's see, it can't be too bad." Joyce cast a brief glance over her shoulder in the direction of the crime scene. "Or at least let's hope it's not, otherwise we might end up on the suspect list."

"Don't even think it." Brenda's lips tightened. She couldn't imagine having to stand up to an interrogation by Detective Crackle. His gruff nature left her pretty intimidated. She shifted her attention to the video on the screen.

Alexa's face appeared first, shrouded by trees, sunlight and what appeared to be an expansive, well-tended park. As she rattled on about the magazine, and how several trucks were in competition to get featured in the magazine, Brenda was drawn in by her casual, yet engaging, attitude. She could see why Melissa enjoyed her vlog. Alexa struck her as the type of person that had a knack for making anything interesting.

When the video shifted from Alexa's commentary to the footage she had taken at the truck, Brenda's muscles tensed in reaction to the sight of herself on camera. Yes, she really had put on weight. No, that hairnet wasn't flattering in the least. Why did her nose keep twitching? With her attention focused on her own looks, she almost missed the verbal exchange. Alexa had included all of her stumbling attempts at speaking, but cut off the video right before she shifted into her more coherent speech. The video cut away to Alexa in the park again. She began to openly mock Brenda for her nervousness.

"Listen up lads and ladies, image sells just as much as delicious donuts. If you can't talk a good game about what you're selling, then many people will never even get to tasting. However, I have to say that I'm glad I did. Although the donut truck left a lot to be desired when it comes to customer service, the donut itself melted in my mouth with a delicious, airy consistency and just enough sweetness to make me want to go back for more. So, according to me, *Donuts on the Move* is definitely a place to go when you have a sweet tooth that needs to be satisfied. Let's just hope that by then, the baker has figured out how to put a sentence together." She laughed then cut off the video feed.

"Ouch." Brenda bit into her bottom lip.

"I know." Melissa sighed. "That's why I didn't want to show it to you."

"Well, to be honest, you were acting pretty foolish. You had nothing to be nervous about." Joyce ducked her head as a smile threatened her lips.

"Thanks, Joyce." Brenda rolled her eyes. "Yes, you're right. And she did actually give a good review of the food. I can see why people loved her, she was very talented."

"Was she, though?" Melissa crossed her arms and shook her head. "I used to think that she was very honest, that's why I liked her. But after watching this, I can't help but wonder if she was in it just for the shock value."

"None of that matters now." Joyce slipped her hands into the pockets of her jacket. "We need to focus on what happened to Alexa. Whether her reviews are honest or not, she still didn't deserve to die. I for one, would like to know who did this."

"I agree." Brenda started to close the webpage, then noticed another video posted just a few hours before the video about *Donuts on the Move*. "Wait, this one looks like it's about *Vanessa's Veggies*. I wonder what she had to say about Vanessa's truck?" She pressed play on the video. Alexa's face appeared, but this time she was framed by the town square. She turned the camera to show Vanessa's truck in front of her.

"So, I've heard a lot of interesting things about

this place. The locals promote it as one of the healthiest places to eat, and insist that it is both vegan and organic, completely chemical free. As you might expect, I'm quite excited to try it out. But I've heard glowing reviews before that didn't pan out to be so great. One bite at a time, right?" She grinned into the camera. A second later that grin faded, and her eyes narrowed. "Or, is it possible that Vanessa is hiding something? Keep an eye out for my next vlog about *Vanessa's Veggies*, perhaps she's not as organic or pure as she claims to be!"

The video cut off. Brenda blinked as she stared at the dark screen.

"She had something against Vanessa?"

"Apparently." Joyce tapped her fingertips along her chin. "Although I don't see how anyone could, she's one of the sweetest people I know."

"I agree." Brenda glanced up at the officers around the crime scene. "I think Detective Crackle should see this video, too." She shared the video with him, then scrolled through the remaining recent vlogs. "Look, there's another one from yesterday. Let's see what it is." She pressed play without waiting to see if any of the others agreed. Her mind whirled with the possible motives behind Alexa's death. Had she given a review that stung so much someone decided to attack her? But if so, why had they dumped her body at the town square? Was it someone that had been reviewed by her, and didn't appreciate her views on things? The thought overwhelmed her. Could they be standing near the killer? She scanned the crowd that continued to grow in the parking lot. A killer might just be hiding in that sea of faces.

CHAPTER 5

Joyce focused on the people in the video and began to lip read right away. It had become a natural instinct for her.

"Here, let me take a closer look. Maybe I'll be able to pick up on some conversations." She peered at the video as it played.

"Can you tell what anyone's saying?" Brenda gazed at her, fascinated by her friend's ability to lip read.

As a child, Joyce had taught herself to lip read. It was a way to protect herself, as her four older brothers were always plotting against her. They had no idea how she figured out their plans, she never breathed a word about her skill to them. Now, she used it in day-to-day life to give herself a little advantage. The things people said when they assumed only certain people could hear them, could be quite eye-opening.

"Not much, no. I'm sorry. People are moving around too much. I can catch a few words, but no full conversations."

As the video played, Alexa came into view. She spoke directly to the gathered protestors.

"We can't stop now. We can't back down. The latest protests we staged against *Garring Farm*, and the grocery chain that the farm supplies, had a huge impact on both businesses. Both reported losses. We are making a difference! Now, we are focusing more on *Country Grocery Place* and its supplier *Marbary Produce Farm*. We will make a difference!" Alexa thrust her hand into the air. "We can be the change that we talk about, we can make it happen. But we have to be one hundred percent dedicated. Some people will lie to us." She swept her gaze across the crowd before turning to the camera. "Some people will pretend to be one way in front of the camera, and then turn out to be totally different! Be careful who you support." She turned back to the crowd and shouted. "We can be the change!"

As the crowd erupted with cheers, the video cut off.

"Wow, she isn't afraid of making enemies, is she?" Joyce frowned.

"No, she's not." Brenda narrowed her eyes. "You know, most of the videos I've seen on Alexa's page have been selfie-style, but clearly this time someone was holding the camera. I wonder who it was?"

"She has friends film for her sometimes." Melissa shrugged. "I don't think it's always the same person, but then again I've never really thought about it."

"Those are two big companies she went after. *Marbary Produce Farm* is one of the largest in the area, and *Country Grocery Place* is opening new stores all of the time. In fact there's a new one opening here next week." Brenda shook her head. "I guess our suspect list isn't going to be short."

"No, it isn't." Joyce frowned as her own phone buzzed. When she pulled it out she saw a new text.

"I just got a text that the magazine's event coordinator, the one that organized the event, is going to make an announcement." Joyce looked up from her phone, her forehead creased. "I'm betting she's going to cancel the rest of it."

"What a shame." Melissa looked between the two women. "I guess there's nothing else she can do, but a lot of people are going to be very disappointed. I wonder if they will still select a winner?"

"I hadn't even thought about that." Brenda tipped her head from side to side. "I suppose they have to since it's a marketing campaign for the magazine. But we might not find out until all of this settles down."

"That's a good point. They may just reschedule everything. Let's head over to the main stage so we can hear the announcement. It looks like that's where everyone is going," Melissa suggested.

"Yes, good idea." Brenda started off in that direction, but kept an eye on Joyce to be sure she followed. Joyce had a tendency to do things her own way, and Brenda sensed that she didn't tell the whole story about her encounter with Detective Crackle. With the possibility of a killer in the crowd with them, she didn't want to lose track of Joyce, or Melissa.

As they joined the crowd of people gathered near the stage, tension filled the air. Those who didn't know exactly what happened were asking questions, others who had been there when Brenda arrived appeared dazed.

"Hello everyone." Angela Jacobsons walked to the center of the stage and looked out at the crowd.

"I'm sorry to announce that there has been a great tragedy. Alexa Vue has been killed. At this time, I don't know much more than that. I don't know the circumstances of her death, or whether anyone else might be in danger. For that reason I think it's best if we cancel the remainder of the event. We will announce who will be featured in the magazine at a later date. Please, cooperate with the police as best you can. They need our help to figure out what happened to Alexa. Thank you for your understanding, and I hope that we can do another event like this sometime soon."

As she left the stage the crowd erupted with questions. However, Angela did not look back. She did not say another word. Instead, she headed straight towards a car that waited for her.

"I guess the magazine is going to want to distance themselves from this as much as possible." Brenda watched the car pull away. "I doubt they're that invested in getting the crime solved."

"They say any publicity is good publicity, but I'm not so sure that applies to murder." Joyce tipped her head towards the stage. "Here comes our favorite detective."

"Can I have everyone's attention please?" He cleared his throat in an attempt to quiet the crowd.

Soon, all eyes were on him. "I want to thank everyone for your cooperation so far. My name is Detective Crackle, and I will be investigating this case. I want all of you to know that any small piece of information you may have could prove to be very valuable. If you have not yet given your statement to one of the officers, then please do. Once you have given your statement, please clear the area so that a thorough crime scene investigation can be done. Again, thank you for your cooperation."

"He does that fairly well." Brenda raised an eyebrow. "I'm impressed."

"Don't be." Joyce rolled her eyes. "I saw him practicing beside the stage. I don't think he's used to having all of the attention on him."

"Probably not. But I'm glad he's the one investigating. I'm sure that he'll get to the bottom of this." Brenda turned towards the flow of the crowd. At the edge of the town square several officers stood with clipboards.

"Maybe with a little help." Joyce nudged her lightly with her elbow. "It never hurts to have extra eyes, right?"

"That's true. But I barely knew Alexa, I'm not sure what we can do to help." Brenda stepped into a line to give her statement to one of the officers.

Joyce stepped up behind her, while Melissa headed off to another line.

"Sometimes not knowing a person allows for a clearer view of who they are and what they are actually like. Maybe Alexa had some secrets from her past that she did a good job of hiding," Joyce said.

Those words played through Brenda's mind as she gave her statement to the officer. He asked for every detail of her morning, from the time she woke up until the time she arrived and saw Alexa's body. She did her best to recount everything, but her thoughts began to blur after some time.

"Ma'am, you said you saw the body, did you see anyone in the car or get back into the car?"

"No, didn't I already answer that?" Brenda narrowed her eyes as she tried to focus on his face. "I turned when I heard a sound, and the car was already driving away."

"So, you're sure you never saw anyone outside the car?" He held his pen poised above his notepad.

"Yes, I'm sure. I can't keep answering the same question, though. I know you're just doing your job, but no matter how many times you ask, the answer isn't going to change." Brenda ran her palm across her forehead in an attempt to clear the fog that had gathered in her mind.

"I understand. We'll be in touch." He stepped aside to allow her to walk past him to the parking lot.

While she waited for Joyce to give her statement, Brenda gazed at the spot that had been roped off in the parking lot. She recalled the moments just before she'd heard the sound and turned to find Alexa's body. They were such normal moments. She couldn't remember her thoughts exactly, but none had to do with murder. Despite the reality of the experience, her thoughts shifted to the needs of the truck. With the event canceled, a day of sales would be lost, and the following day was a day off. It would be a financial hit, but she knew that having the time away from the truck would actually be helpful for all three of them. It would be difficult to return without Alexa on her mind. No, she hadn't been kind to her, and no she didn't feel any genuine connection to the woman, but the loss of her life was still a blow.

"He was quite the eager one, huh?" Joyce shook her head as she joined Brenda in the parking lot. "Do they train these youngsters to ask the same question over and over or do you think he just had a memory problem?"

"I think they probably train them that way."

Brenda sighed as she walked beside Joyce towards her car. "I just wish I had more to tell him. I keep thinking that if I had only turned around faster, I might have seen more. I might have caught a glimpse of the killer."

"You did plenty." Joyce wrapped her in a warm hug. "You called Detective Crackle right away, and you kept the cars from running over evidence. If you weren't there, the police wouldn't have had a head start."

"I guess." Brenda bit into her bottom lip. "I just wish none of this happened."

"I agree with you there." Joyce frowned. "It's a tough thing to handle. But we will get through this. I'm sure that Charlie is worried about you, get home to him." She opened her car door. "We'll check in later, okay?"

"Yes, let's do that." Brenda nodded.

Joyce watched through her rearview mirror as Brenda walked to her car. Despite all the events of the day, Brenda held her head high as she walked. She had a deep strength that Joyce knew she had yet to recognize. She came across as timid, but in the moments that she needed that strength, it was always there.

Joyce steered out of the parking lot, and did her

best not to look back over her shoulder. When she'd first received the texts from Brenda that morning, they had left her shocked. She had hoped that somehow they weren't true. However, now she knew they were. Not only was the event they had planned for so long canceled, but now they were caught up in the middle of a murder investigation.

As Joyce drove through town back towards the small house she had once shared with her husband, she noticed signs that word had spread. Neighbors stood in each others' driveways. Children were kept close, instead of allowed to wander around the block as they usually were. In general, the town was a safe one. However, as a cop's wife, she knew that no town was ever actually completely safe. It might appear to be so on the surface, but there were always dark secrets to be discovered. The illusion of safety was never something she bought into. She also knew that a killer didn't look a certain way, or act a certain way. A killer could be anyone, from the dog groomer, to the mailman.

But who had a reason to kill Alexa? Was it the people that she'd attacked through her vlog? Joyce supported the right of free speech, but at times felt that the younger generation misunderstood what that meant. Yes, they had the right to say anything they pleased, but not without consequence. Words, especially recorded ones, were something that could never be taken back.

Joyce thought about her exchange with Detective Crackle. She didn't really think he was a buffoon, and regretted calling him that. But the sight of him grilling Brenda had sparked a protective streak within her that she couldn't ignore. She and Brenda had forged a close friendship, and in some ways the younger woman felt like a daughter to her. She enjoyed being a part of her, and her family's lives. She missed her children who were now adults and lived on the other side of the country. In just a short time she'd gone from general isolation as she grieved the death of her husband, to being part of a bustling business, and a very loving family. But that wasn't what Detective Crackle saw when he looked at Brenda. He saw the potential for the clue that might just solve the crime. She'd often seen that gleam in Davey's eyes when he investigated a crime. She'd have to remind him that this wasn't just a puzzle to solve, real human lives were involved, and that compassion went a long way.

He didn't always listen. Neither did Detective Crackle. She pulled into her driveway and took a moment to close her eyes. After the crazy morning, she wasn't sure how she would ever settle down. Her mind spun with the possibilities of what might have happened to Alexa. Sure, she may have made some enemies with her vlog, but would that really be enough reason for someone to kill her? She shook her head, then stepped out of the car. Alexa wasn't scared of scandal. She wasn't afraid to go after heavy hitters, like grocery chains and large farms. Perhaps she had just pushed it too far.

Joyce opened her front door, and heard a loud thump from the other room. The sound startled her at first, then she smiled in reaction to it.

"Yes, I'm home, Molly. Hang on, I'm coming to see you." Joyce tugged her shoes off, left them near the door, then headed down the hall to Molly's room. Molly had a hutch so big that it needed a room to itself. It gave the rabbit plenty of space, but most of the time Joyce let Molly roam free and she often managed to escape her hutch. When she did escape it could take Joyce quite some time to find where the rabbit had hidden, and she could leave quite a mess. "Hi baby." She cooed at the rabbit as she opened the door to her hutch. "I'm home early."

Molly practically jumped into her arms. Joyce cuddled her as she carried her into the living room.

The softness of the rabbit's white coat still startled her. She'd never felt anything softer.

As Joyce sat down on the couch with Molly, the rabbit twitched her nose. "Yes, I know, I shouldn't be home, yet. But something terrible happened today." She confided the entire experience to Molly. "If only Davey was here, he'd be able to figure this out, I'm sure of it. But he's not." She glanced over at the picture of her late husband that hung on the wall. She still missed him as much as the first day she lost him, but somehow the pain had gotten a little less sharp over time. She had to admit that sometimes Detective Crackle reminded her of him. Perhaps that was why she felt a faint buzz of excitement each time she saw him. She closed her eyes and attempted to wash that sensation away. Whatever the reason she felt it, it wasn't important at the moment. What mattered was finding out what happened to Alexa, and she certainly wasn't going to leave it solely in the hands of Detective Crackle. She could only guess how many interviews he would have to wade through before he made any progress on the case. She intended to go straight to the source, Alexa's website.

CHAPTER 6

Brenda opened the front door to her house, and released a sigh of relief. Only two hours before she had walked out, eager to get an early start to her day. Now she had returned, with the urge to never leave again. At least at home she knew what to expect, and she felt safe. She had sent a brief text to Charlie to let him know what had happened and that she was fine. The quiet in the house indicated that her daughter and husband might have gone out. But as she stepped farther inside, she heard a voice call out to her.

"Brenda, is that you?"

Charlie stepped out of the hall that led from the living room to the kitchen. The sight of him made her heart lurch with a sudden mixture of emotions. Without saying a word, she opened her arms to him. It took him only a second to reach her. As he wrapped her up in his arms he kissed the top of her head.

"I know. I know it's been a rough morning." Charlie winced.

"I have no idea how this could happen, Charlie." Brenda buried her nose in the curve of his neck, the faint scent of his favorite soap soothed her.

"It's a terrible thing. I sent Sophie over to Dawn's to play so we could have some time alone to talk about what happened." Charlie led her to the couch, then sat down beside her. "Are you okay? There wasn't much said on the news report about what happened, other than a body being found."

"Yes, I am okay. No one else was hurt. But I was there, I saw her, and I just can't get that moment out of my mind, Charlie. I was walking through the parking lot, then I heard something hit the ground, and tires squeal. By the time I turned around the car was almost gone, and Alexa was there." She shuddered at the memory.

"I've said it before, and I mean it. They really need to increase security at these events."

"That's the thing, there was plenty of security. Detective Crackle was even there to make sure that the security was in place, because of the protests they expected. And the protests happened yesterday, and there was a scuffle, but no one got hurt. Except, I did hear a rumor that a punch started the whole thing. Someone snatched Alexa first thing this morning, even before I was up. She was in the middle of a vlog." Brenda sat back and looked into her husband's eyes. "It must have happened so fast. I can't even imagine. She had to have been in her hotel room, how could anyone have access to her there?"

"It must have been someone she trusted." Charlie frowned as he continued to hold her close. "You know, when she worked at the paper for a few weeks she told me about receiving death threats. She claimed she didn't take any of them seriously, but she tended to upset a lot of people."

"Really? Did you get to know her well?" Brenda checked her phone, relieved to see a text from Joyce that she had gotten home safe. "I want you to tell me everything you can about her. I feel like I knew nothing about her, and maybe if I knew a little bit more it would help all of this to make sense."

"I'm sorry, I really didn't know her well. I'm not sure that anyone could know her well. She had such an arrogant nature. I asked her once how she dealt with all of the fame, and she said she had a good friend back home that kept her humble." Charlie closed his eyes, then nodded. "I think her name was Poppy."

"Poppy." Brenda sighed. "I wonder if anyone has been able to reach her friends or family, yet. I hope so."

"I'm sure they would have." He nodded. "What can I do for you? How can I make this better?"

"I'm not sure that you can." She sat down on the edge of the couch, but still held his hand. "I feel like until the killer is found, I'm not going to be able to move on from this."

"The police will figure all of this out." He sat down beside her and leaned close. "I'm here for you, sweetheart, whatever you need. Just say the word, and I'll do it."

"All I need is you, Charlie." She smiled as she gazed at him. "I don't know how I got so lucky."

"I could say the same." He gave her a light kiss on her cheek. "In fact, I should say it more often. Hopefully, all of this will be over soon. I'm sure the police will put all of their resources on this."

"If it's up to Joyce we might not just leave it to the police." Brenda smiled some. "She has such a mind for mysteries, I guess since she spent so many years discussing cases with Davey."

"It probably makes her feel close to him again to investigate things." Charlie's jaw tensed some as he studied her. "I can understand why she would want to investigate, but it's important to be careful. Whoever did this to Alexa, didn't just kill her. The person wanted to send a message. Otherwise why would the body have been left at the town square?"

"That's what I was thinking." Brenda sat forward, her eyes narrowed as she contemplated the options. "Someone wanted her found quickly. I mean why risk dropping her there when there were people already around?" She shivered again as the image replayed through her mind. "You're right, whoever did this is a very dangerous person. We will be careful."

"If their message doesn't get across, then I'm going to bet that they will try to make their point clearer." Charlie ran his hand along his chin and groaned. "This is such a tough situation."

"You know what I really need?" Brenda stood up from the couch.

"What's that?" He stood up as well.

"A hug from Sophie, and the rest of the day with my two favorite people. I'll make us a snack." Brenda headed for the kitchen.

"I'll go get Sophie. Be right back." Charlie stepped out through the front door.

As Brenda put together a platter of crackers, cheese, and green grapes for them all to share, for just a second everything that happened disappeared from her mind. When she heard the door shut, it all came rushing back. Yes, she'd heard the car squeal away. If she could remember all of that, why couldn't she remember the things that mattered? The car? The plate? Anything? She closed her eyes and summoned back those few moments that changed everything. When she opened her eyes again, the sweetest smile greeted her.

"Hi, Mommy!" Sophie flung her arms around her waist.

"Hi, my sweet Sophie." Brenda swept her up into her arms and smothered her cheeks in kisses. "How about a snack and a board game?"

"Yes!" Sophie giggled. The pure joy in her eyes reminded Brenda that although everything might seem pretty dismal, she had plenty to be happy about.

Joyce sat on the edge of her undisturbed bed. She didn't even bother pulling the covers back. She knew that the moment she closed her eyes all that she would think about was Alexa. She'd tried a cup of warm milk and turning on a show that always made her sleepy, but that wasn't enough to even get a doze out of her. Instead, she realized that she could try to get to sleep all night, or she could put her time to use. She'd tried looking through Alexa's website earlier in the day, but hadn't found much. Maybe she'd missed something.

Joyce grabbed her laptop and set it up on the small, wooden desk in her bedroom. Briefly, her mind flashed back to all of the times she'd sit at that desk with her husband. Sometimes they would spread out on the kitchen table, but most of the time they would share the small desk, shoulder to shoulder, while they tried to get to the bottom of one of his cases. Now, it seemed as if there was so much space. The thought made her heart ache for a few seconds before she focused on the computer screen. Davey always told her, if you want to understand the crime, you have to get to know your victim.

Nine times out of ten, the truth could be found in the history or lifestyle of the person who was killed. "Death reveals all of the secrets we thought we kept so well."

Joyce could hear his voice float through the room. She couldn't help but wonder what secrets might be revealed in her own death. But there wasn't time to dwell on that. She needed to focus on the website. It was a direct link to Alexa, her thoughts, her beliefs, and perhaps some of her history. She scrolled through some of the videos, looking for one in particular that she wanted to watch again.

It was Alexa's video about *Vanessa's Veggies* and what Vanessa might be hiding. The way she ended the video made her think that Alexa knew something very juicy about Vanessa. But was that just her way of reeling her viewers in? She decided to re-watch it. As the video played she noticed the gleam in Alexa's eyes. She didn't think that was something that the woman could fake. It seemed to her that she definitely had some dirt on Vanessa. However, the video didn't reveal anything more than that. She closed the video, then began to look through some of the other videos on the site.

Joyce chose the video that showed some of the protests from the day before. With a few clicks she was able to enlarge the video. She wanted to try and lip read.

As Joyce watched the video, she was able to pick up on a few conversations. But since most of the protesters were moving, and the video panned in different directions it was hard to get more than a snippet here and there. After watching the video a few times, she looked for another video she had watched earlier. It was about *Garring Farm*, a dairy farm. After several minutes of searching, she found that it was no longer on the site. Annoyed, she scrolled through a few more of the videos, only to find that some others had gone missing as well, including the video that reviewed *Donuts on the Move*. She sat back in her chair and considered how this might happen. Alexa was already dead when they watched the videos earlier. It's not like she could be deleting them from beyond the grave. So, how were the videos disappearing? Joyce typed out a brief email to Melissa. Perhaps since she was familiar with the site, and Alexa's vlogs, she would have an idea of why it was happening.

Once Joyce had sent it, she refocused on Alexa's

social media. She wasn't up to date on all of the latest trends when it came to the internet or apps, but she knew enough to find a little information on Alexa. From what she could tell, she was no stranger to bad reviews. On several of her sites, there were pages of negative comments, both from restaurants she had reviewed, and people she had upset in other ways. As she read through the assortment of comments, the night slipped away from her. By the time she looked at the clock again it was nearly dawn.

Still not tired, but certainly restless, she picked up her phone. There was only one person she knew that would be up this early. As the phone rang, she hoped that Brenda would be as eager as her to find out what happened to Alexa.

"Hello?" Brenda's voice sounded garbled as she spoke.

"Brenda? Are you sleeping?"

"I was, yes." Brenda coughed and her voice became a bit clearer. "Is everything okay?"

"Yes, I'm so sorry. I just assumed you would be up. You should go back to sleep."

"I'm up, now." Brenda laughed some, then coughed again. "What did you need?"

"I was thinking it might be a good idea to look at

the parking lot again. I'm sure that the police did a thorough search, but it couldn't hurt to take another look, could it?" Joyce frowned as a wave of guilt for waking Brenda up washed over her. Perhaps she should have just gone to look at the parking lot alone.

"Sure, that sounds like a good idea, actually. As quickly as that car moved, I'm sure that something had to be left behind. I only wish that I could remember more."

"Perhaps just being there again will jog your memory. You never know. I will meet you there, in say, about thirty minutes?" Joyce glanced at the clock. "It would have been around the same time the body was dumped. The sun should be coming up shortly after."

"Sure, that sounds fine, I'll be there."

As soon as Brenda hung up the phone, Joyce wondered if she asked too much of her friend. What she'd experienced was upsetting, and putting her back in that same location might be a bad idea. But she knew Brenda well enough to know that if she didn't feel comfortable, she would say something. Brenda would want to try and help solve the crime. They were very similar that way.

After Joyce fed Molly, she made a cup of coffee.

The house was quiet, as always. She turned on the small radio that she kept on the kitchen table. The music kept her company when she needed it. As a familiar song played, she thought about the years that had passed in her life. She didn't feel as if she was in her sixties. She still felt like the young woman that had marched in protests, and proclaimed with determination that she would never marry. And yet, life had taken her in a very different direction. She could only imagine where Alexa expected her life to take her. Perhaps, there were some clues in those expectations. She seemed to be very dedicated to having a media presence, informing her audience about what was contained in the food they ate, and to promoting food that didn't contain harsh chemicals. Maybe, her death was somehow linked with that passion. Could it have been someone seeking revenge for one of her protests, or perhaps someone who thought she wasn't doing enough to promote organic food? She had eaten the non-organic donuts from the truck, so she wasn't strict.

If this wasn't solved soon, Joyce knew it would be important to expand the search to her friends and family. Unfortunately, with her not being local, that would be difficult. But she did have quite a crowd of followers, and as long as they were still in town they might be able to discover something. She drove towards the town square, and hoped that they would stumble over a clue.

CHAPTER 7

*B*renda parked at the edge of the parking lot. There wasn't another car in sight. However, to her, the parking lot was full of all of the memories from the day before. In reality, it was completely empty. Not a piece of paper, or a crumpled-up cup. The police had been quite thorough. She stepped out of the car and began to walk along the perimeter. She had almost made it to the entrance of the town square, before she'd heard the sound behind her that made her turn around. She walked to the same position, facing the town square. As she took a deep breath, she tried to visualize the exact events that unfolded. If anything was going to jog her memory, it would be that. As she took another breath, the sound of a car behind her made her gasp. She spun around, and the headlights of the car nearly blinded her.

"Brenda, are you okay?" The lights shut off as Joyce stepped out of the car. "I'm sorry, I didn't mean to startle you."

"The lights." She stared at the now unlit headlights.

"I know, sorry." Joyce touched her friend's arm. "Are you okay?"

"No, I mean, there were no lights. On the car, when it drove away. The taillights weren't on." Brenda rubbed her eyes, then looked at Joyce. "Why wouldn't there have been lights?"

"I don't know. Maybe they didn't want to draw attention to the car? Maybe they were broken?" She studied her friend with a frown. "Are you sure you're up for this?"

"It's something right? At least I remembered something." Brenda rubbed her hands together, then looked over the parking lot. "There's nothing left here to find."

"Maybe not, but I think we should take a look anyway. Just a second, I've got a text from Melissa." Joyce scrolled through the message, then raised an eyebrow. "I'm going to give her a quick call, I'll be right here."

STRAWBERRY DONUTS AND SCANDAL

"Okay." Brenda nodded, then wandered off to look through the parking lot.

Joyce dialed Melissa's number. She watched her friend walk across the parking lot as the phone rang.

"I thought you might call." Melissa's tense voice echoed in Joyce's ear.

"Can you please explain this all to me? I don't quite understand." Joyce shifted her attention to Melissa's words.

"I took a look at the website. Sometimes vloggers have expiration dates on their videos, they're automatically deleted to keep the content on the site fresh. But that isn't what happened here. Whoever took down those videos, had access to the site. And a few have been removed overnight and this morning. So, clearly it couldn't have been Alexa doing it."

"What would someone need to be able to do that?" Joyce frowned. "I'm not that up to speed with tech."

"All they need is her password, to have access to her site. But as a popular vlogger I'm sure she was very careful about who had it. It's possible if she had anyone helping her manage the site, there could be one or even two other people that have her password." Melissa took a sharp breath. "Wow, one was just deleted a second ago. It's strange, the person isn't wiping the whole site, just random videos."

"Maybe they're not as random as we think." Joyce narrowed her eyes. "Thanks for the information, Melissa."

"Sure, no problem."

As Joyce hung up the phone, Brenda walked back over to her.

"I'm sorry, Joyce, I didn't find anything. The only thing I remembered were the taillights being out." Brenda sighed. "I don't think that's going to help much."

"It might, you never know." Joyce filled her in on the information Melissa gave her. "I'm going to give Detective Crackle a call. He needs to know about the videos, if someone is deleting them on purpose, that means they have access to her account. What do you think that person is trying to hide?" She frowned as she dialed the detective's number.

"I don't know. Was the video of her being abducted deleted?" Brenda pulled out her phone to check for herself.

"I'm not sure." Joyce kept her phone to her ear. After a few rings, Detective Crackle answered.

"Joyce, I was planning to call you."

"I saved you the trouble." Joyce crossed one arm over her stomach and turned away from Brenda as a touch of heat tingled through her cheeks. "Listen, we have reason to believe that there is someone accessing Alexa's website and deleting her vlogs."

"Are you certain about that?" His tone shifted from amiable to sharp.

"Yes. Apparently, some of the vloggers set their videos to automatically delete after a certain amount of time, but the videos being deleted are random. So, it isn't being done automatically. Someone must have access to the site, and whoever does, is deleting these videos. I don't know why, but I'm certain there is a reason." Joyce glanced back at Brenda.

"The video of her abduction is still there." Brenda met her eyes. "Why would the killer skip over that one?"

Joyce relayed the information to Detective Crackle.

"I'll have someone look into it right away. Anything else?" Detective Crackle paused.

"Brenda did recall that there were no taillights on when the car drove away. I'm not sure what that might lead to, but every detail counts, right?" She gave Brenda a brief wink.

"Right. Thanks for the information. I guess it would only be fair for me to share an update with you." Detective Crackle cleared his throat. "We've taken Vanessa into custody."

"Vanessa?" Joyce stammered the name. "But why? She couldn't have done this."

"The video on the website points to her as a suspect, and she doesn't have a solid alibi. Right now, we're just questioning her. Tell Brenda I said thanks for the information." Detective Crackle hung up the phone before she could say another word.

As Joyce tucked her phone into her purse, she turned to face Brenda.

"They've taken Vanessa in for questioning. Can you believe that? This is why I can't just let Detective Crackle investigate this crime. I mean, who in their right mind would ever suspect Vanessa?" Joyce threw her hands into the air. "The man is clueless."

"It is the only lead they have, and we don't have much more to offer." Brenda tucked her phone back into her pocket. "I just wish I had seen something more useful."

"You did see something useful, Brenda. Don't be down on yourself about that. You saw everything that was there to see. It's not your fault the car looked too common to narrow down what car it might have been. Detective Crackle said to thank you for the information. Look, I don't think we're going to discover much more by standing here. Why don't we grab some breakfast from the coffee shop? I think it would do us both some good to have something in our stomachs."

"Yes, you're probably right. I haven't been hungry since all of this happened, but that doesn't mean that I don't need to eat." Brenda gritted her teeth. "No matter what, I'm sure that I'm going to need my strength."

"Yes, you will, we both will." Joyce started walking towards their cars.

"It's so quiet here when nothing is happening." Brenda passed a glance back over her shoulder. "It's hard to believe that it was such a busy place only a short time ago."

"I wonder how long it will be before the next event takes place. Now that the police have wrapped up the crime scene, I suppose it's just a matter of time." Joyce reached her car and opened the door.

"It'll be strange when they do have the next event. But people do tend to forget pretty easily." Brenda opened her car door, then met Joyce's eyes.

"At least they will if the murder is solved. If not, then it may take a little longer."

"Oh, it's going to be solved." Joyce raised an eyebrow. "I intend to make sure of that."

Brenda couldn't help but smile to herself as she settled in the driver's seat. Joyce had a way of making her feel as if she could accomplish anything. It was that grit and determination that had finally convinced her to take the leap and work with Joyce in the food truck. She always felt braver around Joyce, who had become one of her closest friends. She was like family. Still, it was hard for her to believe that they could really figure out what happened to Alexa. If the police had so little to go on, then what leads did they have a chance of finding?

∼

Joyce waited for Brenda at the front door of the coffee shop. The morning sun had faded some behind thick clouds. It was a gray morning, which seemed appropriate. When Brenda pulled into the parking lot Joyce waved to her, then held the door open for her.

"Some food for our brains will help us to figure all of this out."

"I hope so. On the way over I've been playing with the idea of Vanessa being involved. She was there when Alexa was left in the parking lot, so if it was her, she must have had an accomplice." Brenda sat down at an empty table, barely aware of the crowded coffee shop around her.

"It couldn't possibly be Vanessa." Joyce shook her head as she sat down across from Brenda. "She'd never hurt a fly. In fact, I remember seeing her one day shooing a fly out of her truck. I offered her some fly paper, and she was horrified by the idea. She said all you have to do is talk to the fly, and they understand, eventually." She smiled as her gaze grew distant. "I found it a little strange then, but now I realize it just proves that she could never hurt Alexa."

"But that video could be pretty damning evidence." Brenda nodded to the waitress as she walked over. "I'll have a coffee please, with cream."

"Tea for me, thanks." Joyce grimaced. "I've been up all night, I really shouldn't have any more coffee."

"Oh, Joyce you didn't tell me that." Brenda

frowned and placed one hand over hers. "That's not good for your health, you know?"

"I'm in my sixties, Brenda, not my grave." She smiled and pulled her hand back. "I couldn't sleep. I couldn't stop thinking about Alexa, and who might have done this to her. And, if I'm being honest, Davey."

"Do you miss discussing cases with him?"

"Yes, and everything else about him. He would always tease me about how determined I would get over his cases. I wouldn't let him rest." A smile crept across her lips. "I would drive the poor man crazy. But the truth is, the moment I let up, he would show that he was just as determined."

"I bet he loved every minute." Brenda took her friend's hand again, and this time, Joyce didn't pull back from her touch. "You know if you ever can't sleep, you can always call me."

"Thanks, Brenda. You're such a good friend to me." She gave her hand a light squeeze. "But enough about that. What we need to figure out is, who did this?"

"I doubt it was Vanessa. She just doesn't seem like a killer. Yes, that video looked incriminating, but we still don't even know what Alexa had on her.

Maybe it was nothing." Brenda shook her head. "It doesn't make sense that it could be her."

"No, it doesn't. Who else was in the parking lot? Didn't you say Kevin was there, too?" Joyce accepted her cup of tea from the waitress. "Thank you."

"Oh, one more cream, please." Brenda smiled as she took her cup of coffee. Then she looked back across the table at Joyce. "Sure, Kevin was there. And he has quite a temper. I don't think we can rule him out, that's for sure. There was a man that I don't think I've seen before. But things happened so fast, I could be wrong. I wasn't exactly looking at the other people."

"Yes, Kevin certainly does have a temper. Would he really have been angry enough to kill, though? Even though he has a temper he didn't go after Detective Crackle. He didn't snap and throw a punch." Joyce tipped her head from side to side. "I suppose it's possible, though. I did interrupt before things could get too out of hand."

"You interrupted an argument between Detective Crackle and Kevin?" Brenda raised an eyebrow. "That doesn't seem wise."

"Detective Crackle seemed to agree with that." Joyce winced. "But it felt like a good idea at the time. The point is, I wasn't afraid of Kevin. I would think if he was a killer, I would have been a little afraid."

"It's not easy to spot a killer." Brenda frowned. "I think Kevin is still a possibility, but he would need an accomplice as well. When we find out who is deleting the videos, that will give us more of a direction to look in. Until then, I think we need to consider that we simply have no leads." Brenda sighed. "Not any that are actually leading anywhere, anyway."

"Maybe." Joyce put a finger to her lips as she looked in the direction of a table not far from them. It was crowded with faces she recognized from the town square. After a second she realized they had been part of the protest. The coffee shop was a little noisy, but she could hear some of their conversation, and with her lip reading skills she was able to pick up on bits and pieces.

"What about Alexa?" the young woman spoke. "Someone killed her!"

"So what?" the young man said. "Alexa was a hypocrite. We all know it. So she's dead, we need new leadership, better leadership. At least my vlogs are hard-hitting."

"How can you be so cold about it?" the first

woman said. She took a breath, then nodded. "Mark, we are devastated."

"It doesn't matter, we need to move on," Mark said sternly. "We need to focus on the next protest. We need a voice that's genuine, not a voice that can be bought and sold!"

"Let's at least bury Alexa first." The young woman cringed.

"Enough!" Mark shouted at her. Brenda turned suddenly in his direction. She recognized him in that moment, as one of the protestors. He began to speak in a softer tone.

"What is he saying? Can you tell?" Brenda leaned closer to Joyce. "He was one of the protestors, and I saw him at the truck with that girl who refused to buy our donuts because they weren't organic."

"I think I also recognize him from when Alexa was filming," Joyce said. "He was with her when she got the donuts from you."

"Really, I didn't notice."

"You wouldn't have, you were focusing on the camera." Joyce smiled. "He was in a group of people standing behind Alexa."

"Which means they might know something." Brenda focused in on Mark. "We need to find out

CINDY BELL

what that is."

"Yes, we do, and it looks like they're getting their check. I guess we're going to have to skip breakfast." Joyce took the last swallow of her tea.

"I wasn't hungry anyway." Brenda pushed aside her coffee mug and left enough cash on the table to cover the bill and a tip.

Mark stood up from the table, his shoulders tight.

"I have somewhere to be." He tossed a wadded up bill on the table, then turned and headed for the door. As the others remained at the table, Brenda led Joyce after Mark and right out into the parking lot. He rounded the corner of the building and headed into the rear lot. Brenda and Joyce matched his pace, though a few steps behind.

"What is the plan here?" Joyce grabbed Brenda's shoulder before she could get too far ahead of her. "It's not like he's just going to spill his guts."

"I don't know, he seemed to have a lot to say in the coffee shop. He seems to like an audience. Maybe he'll be willing to talk." Brenda kept her gaze locked on him as he headed for his car.

"You're right. I also recognize him from the videos of the protest. I bet he knows who threw the first punch that got everything stirred up. He definitely has a temper. We need to be careful." Joyce stepped ahead of Brenda. "And we need to catch him before he gets in his car."

Brenda chased after her, determined not to let her friend get out of reach. Just as Mark opened the door to his car, he spun around to face them both.

"What are you two doing following me?"

CHAPTER 8

A chill bolted up Brenda's spine as she looked straight into Mark's cold blue eyes. She hadn't expected him to confront them, but if she was honest with herself, they hadn't been very careful as they followed him.

"Mark, right?" Joyce stepped in front of Brenda and smiled. She could guess from his smooth skin, that he had yet to hit his thirties. The young man shifted his attention to her, and she faced the harshness of his expression.

"How do you know my name? What do you want?" Mark slammed the door of his car shut. "You don't have any business following me around."

"I'm so sorry." Joyce waved her hand in front of her face and sighed. "It's just that we're such big fans of your work, and we wanted a minute to speak with you, but my friend here, she's so shy." She glanced over at Brenda. "Isn't that right? She didn't want to bother you. But I told her, you wouldn't mind, because we all share the same passion, right?"

"What are you talking about?" Mark frowned, but his gaze softened some.

"We've seen your videos," Brenda stumbled over her words. It wasn't hard for her to play shy, she was already quite nervous. "We're so glad that someone finally has the courage to speak the truth."

"Instead of selling out." Joyce rolled her eyes. "I can't tell you how many times I've written out checks to people who claim to fight for our right to eat clean food, only to find out later that they're just putting on a show for the cameras. I mean, how can anyone be so duplicitous?"

"You've seen my videos." He smiled some. "They don't get as many views as others. People don't like it when you don't sugarcoat the truth."

"We do." Brenda nodded. "Real change can't happen if you don't tell the actual truth."

"Absolutely." Joyce grinned. "I'm sorry, I'm a little starstruck. Do you have just a few minutes to talk with us? Oh, we'd love to hear where the next protest will be. We missed this last one, and I can't tell you how much I regret it!"

"I made us miss it." Brenda lowered her eyes as her shoulders slumped. "I thought it was going to be the day after. I don't know how I got so mixed up."

"It's all right. That protest wasn't planned. Well, it was, but it was just a publicity stunt for Alexa. She didn't care about the issue, she just wanted to take advantage of all of the media being around. When I tried to speak some truth, things got a little tense. But that's how real protests go. Sometimes things get a little messy. They turn into a scandal."

"Oh wow, that must have been so exciting." Joyce regarded him for a moment. "Honestly, I was a little surprised to discover that you were associated with Alexa Vue. She seemed a bit well, I'm not sure what the polite way to put it is."

"Fake?" He nodded. "You're right. I was planning to part ways with her, but clearly that won't be necessary now. She was becoming more of an obstacle than a help."

"You must be a little relieved that she's gone." Brenda smiled a little. "It's okay, you can tell us."

"Relieved that she's dead?" He looked between them, then shrugged. "I wouldn't say that. But I am glad that she's no longer in the way. Now, maybe we can make some progress towards some real change. The next protest will be at the grand opening of *Country Grocery Place*, tomorrow. I expect to see you both there."

"*Country Grocery Place?*" Brenda raised an eyebrow. "Is this about *Marbary Produce Farm?*"

"Yes, it is. Alexa was supposed to do a big exposé about the grocery chain, and the farm, but she decided against it at the last minute. My guess is she was paid off." He rolled his eyes. "Just like so many others. But I'm not backing down. I'm going to make sure that they are exposed for all of the chemicals they are pouring into our food." He reached up and scratched at his collar.

Joyce noticed a long scratch from the curve of his chin to the slope of his shoulder.

"Will it be dangerous?" She locked eyes with him.

"It may be." Mark stared back into her eyes. "But if you're afraid of danger, then you're afraid of change."

"We'll be there." Joyce smiled. "Thanks for all that you do, Mark. You're a true hero."

"Somebody has to be." Mark jerked the door open to his light blue, four-door car and climbed in.

Brenda and Joyce stepped out of the way as he

backed the car up, then pulled out of the parking lot.

"What an intense kid." Joyce shook her head. "He's so young to be so angry."

"He has a cause." Brenda crossed her arms. "But I'm not so sure it's protecting our food."

"What do you mean?" Joyce walked beside her as they started back towards the front parking lot.

"I mean it seems to me that he's more interested in attention, and if that's the case, then perhaps he had a big problem with Alexa having so much of it." Brenda paused beside her car. "I think there's a good chance that Mark wanted Alexa out of the picture."

"I agree."

"His car could have been the one I saw when Alexa's body was dumped. But I thought it was darker."

"Did you see that scratch on his neck?" Joyce raised an eyebrow. "I wonder if that came from the fight at the protest."

"It could have. But maybe Alexa scratched her killer?" Brenda watched as her friend tried to hide a yawn. "Before we do anything else, you need to get home and get some rest. All right?"

"Yes, I think I could use a nap." Joyce shivered

a bit as she recalled the way that Mark looked into their eyes. "We have to protest tomorrow, after all."

"Joyce, you can't be serious. You saw how the protest erupted at the town square. It won't be safe for us to be there. You're very brave I know that, but I'm afraid I have to draw the line here. We have no idea just how dangerous Mark could be."

"I see." Joyce smiled as she met her eyes. "Well, I suppose, if you've drawn the line, there's nothing I can do about it."

"Joyce, I'm serious." Brenda searched her expression for some sign that she understood.

"I know you are. I'm just going to go home and take a nap. What kind of trouble could I get into?" Joyce gave Brenda a quick hug. "Make sure you actually eat something, all right?"

"Sure. It's not as if I couldn't stand to lose a few pounds." Brenda glanced down at her stomach.

"Stop that." Joyce gave her a light swat on the shoulder. "You're a beautiful woman, and you are perfect just as you are, and I'm sure that Charlie would agree. He'd also agree that you need to eat something, so get to it, or I'll let him know that you've been skipping meals."

"You two would team up on me." Brenda winced, then smiled at her friend. "Don't worry, I'll make sure that I eat something. You make sure that you actually sleep."

"Will do." Joyce waved as she headed for her car.

Brenda climbed into her own car. Even though she wasn't hungry she decided to head home and see if Charlie and Sophie wanted to grab something to eat. As she turned on the engine, she got a text from Charlie explaining that he was with Sophie at the farmers market. She loved spending time with them, so she decided to join them. As she drove out of the parking lot, she caught sight of Joyce pulling out behind her. To her relief, she turned in the direction of her house. Maybe, she really would get some sleep.

~

Joyce drove towards her house with every intention of taking a nap. However, when she stopped at a red light, she looked over at the diner and she suddenly felt very hungry. She had just decided to turn in when a horn blared behind her.

Joyce waved a hand through the window at the person behind her, and drove through the intersection. As she pulled into the parking lot of the diner, she noticed Detective Crackle's beat-up car. She pulled into a parking spot, and put the car into park.

As she looked at Detective Crackle's car, she realized that she was excited by the prospect of seeing him. That wasn't like her at all.

Joyce flipped down the mirror on her visor to check the state of her hair and the light make-up she wore. Everything appeared to be in place. She flipped the mirror closed again and did her best to pretend that she hadn't checked at all.

"Don't be ridiculous, Joyce, he won't even notice you." She headed towards the door of the diner. She was relieved to see that there weren't too many people inside. If she managed to talk with Detective Crackle, she certainly didn't want their encounter to become the talk of the town. It didn't take long to spot him, he had chosen a table in the center of the diner. She found herself relieved to find that no one was sitting in the only other chair at the table. Was he waiting for someone? It was none of her business. She took a breath, reminded herself to do her best to be polite, then walked over to him.

"Detective." She paused beside the table.

"Joyce." Detective Crackle seemed shocked to see her. He stood up and smiled as he greeted her. "I am having a late breakfast. Why don't you join me?"

He cleared his throat. "Unless you are meeting someone."

Joyce didn't know what to do. She wanted him to ask her and now she wasn't sure of the best thing to do.

"I don't want to intrude."

"Not at all." Detective Crackle gestured to the chair and smiled. "Take a seat."

"Thank you!" Joyce sat down across from him and smiled in return. She did her best to ignore the subtle skip of her heartbeat. It was nothing more than a meal, she reminded herself.

"I'll just be a second." Detective Crackle stood up, walked over to the waitress and talked to her softly. His back was to Joyce, so she couldn't see what he was saying. He turned around, walked back to her and sat down.

"Let's order. Oh, and before you try to squabble with me, I'll be covering the check." He lofted an eyebrow as he met her eyes.

"Squabble?" Joyce laughed. "I would never. However, I am perfectly capable of paying for my own breakfast."

"Enough." He shook his head. "This is not up for debate. If a lady joins me for a meal, I pay the check. I've already spoken to the waitress, it's settled."

"Hmm, you went to a lot of trouble." Joyce smiled as she picked up the menu to look through, really she wanted to use it to hide behind. She never knew what to expect with him.

"I have to with you, that much I've learned." He eyed her over the top of the menu. "Without a little planning, I doubt that I could ever win an argument with you."

"Oh, you haven't won, but I'll let you think you have." Joyce set her menu down and looked across the table at him. "Aren't we both a little too old for games?"

"I wouldn't know." He folded his hands. "I haven't felt old a day in my life. Have you?"

The question caught Joyce off guard. When she passed sixty, she'd settled into the idea that people would see her as 'older'. She could still avoid elderly, but she'd accepted that her new label was 'older'. However, the label never felt right to her. There wasn't a moment in her life that she'd felt as if she'd somehow passed into a new stage. She didn't feel much different as she sat across from Detective Crackle, than she did when she sat across from her husband on their first date. Age only seemed to happen physically. But she still felt the same mentally.

"No, I suppose I haven't." She smiled some, and was about to say more, but another voice cut into the conversation before she could.

"Hi there, Joyce." Jackie leaned against the table and smiled. "I see you have company today. Well, company other than Brenda."

"Yes, for once." Joyce spared the waitress a smile. Jackie was sweet, but she could also be very nosy. As she placed her order, she noticed the way that Jackie looked between her and Detective Crackle.

"And what are you going to have, Arthur?" Jackie leaned closer to him.

Arthur? Joyce glanced towards the window to hide her surprise. Not only did Jackie know the detective, but apparently she was on a first name basis with him. Detective Crackle had told Joyce to use his first name, but she still thought of him as Detective Crackle, not Arthur, so rarely used it. Once he'd given his order, he turned his attention back to Joyce.

"Actually, now that I've got you here, I wanted to ask you a few questions." Detective Crackle folded his hands on the table.

"You do?" She smiled a bit. "Fire away."

"What do you know about Vanessa?"

"Vanessa?" Joyce frowned. "Nothing really, she just runs *Vanessa's Veggies*. She is a lovely person."

"So, you don't think she would hurt Alexa."

"Never, why?" Joyce looked into his eyes. "Oh no, you still think she might have done this."

"She is our main suspect." He held up his hands as if he expected an attack.

"That's ridiculous." Joyce rolled her eyes. "She's harmless. You've got this whole thing twisted."

"Now wait a minute, you didn't even give me a chance to tell you why she's our main suspect. You know that pesky thing we like to call evidence?" His eyes narrowed. "Or are you so convinced that you know everything, not even evidence will change your perspective?"

"What evidence could you possibly have against her? Something more than that video, I hope. That was likely some publicity stunt, she just never got to finish it, unfortunately." Joyce frowned as Jackie returned to the table with their food. "Thank you, Jackie."

"Do you have everything you need, Arthur?" Jackie winked at him.

"Yes, thanks." Detective Crackle barely looked

away from Joyce to nod at her. As soon as Jackie walked away, he leaned closer to her. "The video wasn't a publicity stunt. Alexa really did plan to expose something about Vanessa. Vanessa had recently agreed to a deal with the grocery chain *Country Grocery Place*. Part of this agreement included her agreeing to use their suppliers, which would ultimately mean that she would need to get most of her produce from *Marbary Produce Farm*." He paused as he held her gaze, waiting for her to make the connection.

"The farm that's been using the pesticides everyone is protesting against?" Joyce gasped, which drew the attention of a few people around her. Once they'd lost interest, she lowered her voice. "Vanessa claims that her food is vegan, and one hundred percent organic. That kind of information getting out would have been a huge scandal. It would have ruined her."

"You're right. Which is why she has the strongest motive to commit the murder." Detective Crackle picked up his fork. "Now, what do you think, is it still ridiculous?"

"Maybe not." Joyce dug into her plate of food. "But I'm not convinced. Just because she has motive, doesn't mean that she did it. Besides,

Alexa never followed through with publishing the video."

"Because she never had the chance. Vanessa had the motive, she had the opportunity as well, as according to her she'd arrived early at the town square to meet Alexa. She claims that Alexa never arrived. But one theory is that perhaps Vanessa abducted Alexa, then had someone else drive the car and dump the body. It's the perfect way to give herself an alibi, and make a statement." Detective Crackle pursed his lips as he tilted his head from side to side. "It's certainly not a slam dunk, but it's a place to start."

"Maybe." Joyce winced as she considered the possibility. "I hate to think it, but I honestly don't know her that well."

"I intend to get to know her very well." Detective Crackle met her eyes. "I can assure you, Joyce, it isn't my intention to put an innocent woman behind bars. The evidence will prove who did this."

"Let's hope so." Joyce settled back in her chair. Knowing that Detective Crackle was so determined to get to the truth, did reassure her.

CHAPTER 9

After spending a couple of hours at the farmers market, Brenda left Charlie and Sophie there. They had decided that Brenda would pick up lunch for the whole family and they would meet at home. She knew she needed to eat, even though she didn't feel hungry. There was one thing she couldn't turn down, no matter how little appetite she had. Brenda headed straight for the shopping district downtown. She knew Kevin would have his truck parked there. Maybe, she could get a little information to go along with his delicious burgers.

As Brenda approached Kevin's truck, the smell of his famous burgers was tantalizing. For the first time since Alexa's death, her stomach rumbled with the desire to eat. She joined the short line of customers, and watched as each one walked away from the window with a big smile.

"Hey Brenda." Kevin smiled at her when she reached the window. "What are you doing out here? I thought it was your day off?"

"It is." She smiled in return. "But I'm starving, and only one of your burgers will do."

"You're in luck, I have plenty. Want some fries, too?" He turned around to flip the burgers, then turned back to face her.

"Sure, fries sound good. I'll need three burgers, please." She took a deep breath of the scented air, then sighed in anticipation. "How are you doing, Kevin?"

"So far so good. You know, still a little rattled. It's hard not to be after what we saw." He turned around to drop the fries in the fryer, then shook his head. "I haven't been able to get it off my mind, to tell you the truth."

"Me either." Brenda studied each motion he made. Despite Kevin's large size he had a certain grace about him that surprised her. Perhaps it was from so many years of running the truck. "Did you know her, Kevin?"

"Alexa?" Kevin turned back to Brenda. "Can't say that I did. I mean, I saw her that day. She tried to shove her phone in my face. I told her I wasn't interested." He chuckled. "You should have seen how offended she was that I turned her down."

"Why did you? She's pretty popular, an interview with her could have been good for your business." Brenda reached into her purse and pulled out her wallet.

"Oh, no charge." Kevin smiled. "Us truckers have to stick together you know."

"Thanks, Kevin." She dropped a few dollars in the tip jar.

"The thing with these techie types, they love to put all their videos everywhere, but sometimes it attracts the wrong kind of people. I don't want a bunch of picky customers asking me about hormones and pesticides. I mean, sure I buy quality meat, but I can't tell you what the cow ate. Some of these people are a little too crazy for me. Besides, I don't need a vlogger to get customers, word of mouth does just fine. As long as I make good food, I get good customers." He clapped his hands together. "It's as simple as that."

"That makes sense. I guess I can see your point. She was involved in protests about pesticides used on *Marbary Produce Farm*." The aroma of the burger cooking reminded her of the delicious flavoring that only Kevin seemed able to master. "I'm sure many of her followers are interested in those topics."

"My point exactly. I don't need that kind of trouble. I don't want a group of kids parading around my truck with signs demanding I go organic or something." He chuckled. "That's never going to happen."

"It's hard to keep up with all of the trends, that's for sure. I bet she didn't like you not wanting to be filmed. She seemed a little pushy."

"Oh, she had quite a mouth." Kevin narrowed his eyes. "People like that usually do."

"People like that?" Brenda leaned against the truck and listened closely to be sure she heard him correctly.

"You know, the ones that always want some kind of attention. If you don't say what they want you to, they'll just put words in your mouth, there's no winning with them. What do I care about pesticides? Nothing. It's a food truck, not a health food store."

"That's true, and it's hard to keep track of what is okay, and not okay." Brenda sighed as she shook her head. "I'm always thinking about what my daughter is eating and whether it's completely safe. But it seems impossible to know."

"It seems that way, because it is." Kevin grunted. "People waste too much time on that nonsense. Listen, I know it makes me old, and out of touch, but there's a time and a place for everything." He leaned through the window and lowered his voice. "A crowded place, and protests, that's never a good combination. Just like I expected, things got out of hand. But it wasn't just because of the chaos, it was one of the protestors, and Alexa, that stirred things up. I saw it for myself." He shook his head. "It could have gotten really messy, but they didn't care. They just wanted to draw the attention of all of the news' crews."

"You think Alexa and one of the protestors made things escalate on purpose?" Brenda's eyes widened at the thought. It was one thing to plan a protest, but quite another thing to intentionally stage a riot.

"I believe it, yes. Luckily, the police were there to stop it. I can't imagine what would have happened if things had gotten out of hand. People could have really been hurt. I'll be honest with you, Brenda, no one deserves to be murdered, but Alexa wasn't the saint she made herself out to be, and if someone killed her, I wouldn't look much further than the people that were standing beside her." He tipped his head back inside the truck.

Brenda considered his words as he packaged up the chips and burgers.

"Good luck with business today."

"Thanks." He turned to take care of another customer.

As Brenda walked back to her car, she pictured the crowd on the day of the protests. Kevin had a point. If things had gotten out of control a lot more people could have been hurt. Without the increased police presence, that could have easily happened. Kevin's comment played on her mind. What if it was someone close to Alexa who had killed her? Clearly, there was no love lost between her and Mark, perhaps he was involved in her death. As she drove past all of the familiar places on the way to her house, she realized that despite the murder, the town was getting back to normal. Without proper attention the crime could easily get swept under the rug as the community collectively moved on. No, Alexa wasn't liked by everyone, but she had many followers who needed answers.

As Brenda pulled into her driveway, she decided that she would review all of the footage from the protest again. She wanted to see if there was any truth to Kevin's claim, and she also wanted to pay close attention to who might have been close to

Alexa. Was her entourage as loyal as she thought? Mark had turned on her, and if he could have such a poor opinion of her, then what about her other friends? Perhaps the enemy that wanted to end her life was closer than she ever realized.

When Brenda stepped into the house, she found that Sophie and Charlie weren't back yet. She sighed and decided to do a little research while she waited for them. With Alexa's murder on her mind she was having trouble focusing on anything else.

As Brenda settled on the couch with her computer, she felt the pressure build up within her, a need to get to the truth. As she began to look through the videos, she noticed the familiar crowd around Alexa. However, she didn't see anything new. She decided to shift gears and check the videos on local news sites. As she sifted through them, one in particular drew her attention. It took place just before the protest became violent, and appeared to be a general pan over the crowd. However, it caught a moment that surprised her. Mark and Alexa stood close to each other, Mark pointed towards someone on the other side of the crowd, as Alexa turned to look, a woman with bright red hair walked up between them. She shoved Mark so hard that he stumbled. Alexa turned back and grabbed the woman by the arm. Then the camera shifted in the direction of a fight that erupted exactly where Mark had pointed. Brenda replayed the video. She remembered talking to the redheaded woman at the donut truck, she had stood out not only because of her hair, but because she refused to eat the donuts because they weren't organic. She decided to send the link to Joyce. With her lip reading skills, she might just be able to figure out what was said. Just as she hit send Charlie and Sophie came through the door.

~

Joyce closed her front door and leaned back against it with a yawn. Her meal with Detective Crackle left her a little uncertain of what to think about his intentions. But the information he'd given her left her with a mission. If Vanessa was the main suspect, then the best thing she could do was prove that right or wrong. After she picked up Molly from her hutch, she headed straight for her bedroom. She wouldn't be any help to anyone without a nap. As she stretched out in bed, Molly snuggled up next to her. She stroked the rabbit's long, white ears.

Joyce closed her eyes and her thoughts filled

with possibilities. Mark obviously had a bone to pick with Alexa, and so did Vanessa. But Alexa had likely angered several other people as well, from local farmers to big grocery chains. The only thing that made her murder seem personal and specific, was the fact that her body was delivered to the town square. That made it local, that made it a message. But what was the message, and who was it for?

As Joyce started to fall asleep, her mind continued to spin. By the time she woke up it was dark. It took her several seconds to figure out what day it was, and why she had fallen asleep fully dressed. As she sat up in bed, she heard Molly darting around the room. Still sleepy, she picked up her phone and saw that she had a message from Brenda. She played the video she had sent. Right away she saw what Brenda noticed. Who was that woman that Alexa grabbed? Why had she attacked Mark? She played the video again, this time she watched the movement of Mark's lips. Alexa mostly had her back to the camera. Mark pointed across the crowd. After watching it a few times and filling in the blanks she managed to work out what he was saying.

"There he is, he's going to throw the first punch."

Joyce's heart sank. So, they did know the protest was going to turn violent. It sounded as if Mark knew who was going to start the fight, and might have even hired the person to do so. Her muscles tensed at the thought. As far as she knew, in her protesting days, the intent had been pure. These days it seemed as if in many cases the goal was to cause a scandal, so the instigator would be an internet sensation rather than get anything changed for the good of the people. Alexa didn't seem to be trying to stop him. From her body language, she appeared to be in agreement with Mark. Then the redheaded woman came up and shoved Mark hard. It wasn't a playful moment, it was a moment of overflowing fury. So, why was she so angry at him? Who was she? After watching the video a few more times, she decided to switch over to Alexa's website. Perhaps she could put a name to the redheaded woman. As she skimmed through some of the videos, she noticed that no more had been deleted. She sent a quick text to Detective Crackle.

Did you find out who deleted the videos from Alexa's website?

For a moment she stared at her phone. Then she realized it was silly of her to expect him to text back right away. He might be in the middle of something very important. She turned her attention back to the website. The redheaded woman Brenda had served at the donut truck was in a few of the videos, but it wasn't until she got to an older one stored in the archives section that she heard her name. In the video Alexa stood at the front of a group of protestors that held signs declaring the dangers of the particular pesticide they protested against. She began to give a speech, then the redheaded woman stepped out of the crowd behind her and leaned in close to Alexa to whisper something in her ear.

"Are you sure, Poppy?"

The redheaded woman nodded. Then Alexa turned her attention back to the camera.

"I've just received an update that *Garring Farm* has agreed to discontinue the use of these harmful pesticides!"

A cheer erupted in the crowd. Alexa grabbed Poppy's hand and thrust it into the air as the pair joined in the cheers as well.

"Poppy." Joyce narrowed her eyes. She jotted down the name, then placed a call to Brenda. When her friend answered, the tone of her voice warned her that something was amiss.

"Brenda, is everything okay?"

"Yes, sorry. I'm just trying to get dinner together. I'm feeling a little frustrated."

"What's going on?" Joyce frowned.

"I got wrapped up in doing some research about this case, got behind on dinner, Sophie's a little cranky, Charlie got a last-minute article, so now he's on a deadline, things are just a little tense."

"I'm sorry to hear that. I can call back later."

"No, please don't." Brenda sighed. "I need someone to talk to who understands all of this. Charlie is so patient, but I don't think he understands why I'm so focused on this. I need this to be settled so I can move on. You understand don't you, Joyce?"

"Yes, I do. I think that Mark instigated the violence at the protest, and we have someone new that we should look into. A girl named Poppy."

"Poppy? Wait a minute, Charlie mentioned that name to me I think. Charlie? Charlie!"

Joyce pulled the phone away from her ear as Brenda yelled for her husband. When she put it back to her ear, she heard a brief conversation between Brenda and Charlie, followed by Brenda turning her attention back to her. "Yes, Alexa mentioned to Charlie that she had a good friend who kept her grounded. A girl named Poppy."

"Aha, okay so we know they were close. At least at one point. Why Poppy shoved Mark, I have no idea. Clearly, she is here in town, or she was at the time of the video. I'm going to see if I can track down where she might be staying." Joyce smiled as she heard Sophie in the background demanding her mother's attention. "I'll take care of this, Brenda, you have a lot on your plate right now. We can touch base in the morning at the truck."

"Thanks, Joyce. See you tomorrow."

As soon as Joyce hung up the phone, it began to ring. Detective Crackle's name bounced across the screen.

"Hello?"

"Joyce, I just saw your text."

"Oh right, about the videos?"

"Yes. I do have some news for you on that. Do you have a few minutes?"

"Yes, of course." She scooped Molly up and settled her in her lap. "What did you find out?"

"The techies were able to identify a man named Mark Coville as the one who logged into the site at the time the videos were deleted."

"Mark? He's one of the protestors."

"Yes, I know. A ring leader." He paused. "Wait, how did you know that?"

"Brenda and I overheard him talking at the coffee shop, and we spoke to him after." Joyce frowned. "He's obsessive about all of this."

"We've been on the hunt for him, but unfortunately we haven't been able to locate him. If you see him again, please let me know."

"Absolutely, I will. He was quite upset with Alexa, said she wasn't honest about her support, and basically he was glad she was out of the picture." Joyce shuddered at the thought of Mark attacking Alexa. "I also have another name you might want to look into, she's a friend of Alexa's. Her name is Poppy. She was also at the protest. I don't know her last name yet, but according to Brenda's husband, Charlie, she was a good friend of Alexa's."

"Charlie? How is he involved in all of this?" Detective Crackle's tone grew a little tense. "Did he know Alexa?"

"He'd met her briefly in the past. Alexa worked at the newspaper for a couple of weeks a long time ago. But she mentioned Poppy to him then."

"So, he did know her?"

"Detective Crackle, don't let anything get into your head. There's no way Charlie had anything to do with any of this." She frowned as she recognized the determination in his voice.

"Anyone who had contact with Alexa is a potential suspect, Joyce. Of course I don't think he harmed her, but I will need to speak to him about it. I'll look into Poppy as well."

"Now is not the best time, he's on a deadline."

"Joyce, it's my job to ask questions whether it's a good time or a bad time. Thanks for the information."

"Wait, Detective—" Joyce winced as the call cut off. Guilt hammered through her mind as she realized that Brenda and Charlie might be getting a visit from the detective in the middle of a chaotic evening, and it was all because of her. Frustrated, she decided she had to find Poppy. She might just be the key to unraveling the case, and the sooner that happened, the better.

CHAPTER 10

The knock on the door came just after Brenda pulled Sophie, unhappily out of the bathtub.

"I want to play more!" Sophie sniffled.

"We have to get you dried off and into your pajamas, it's getting late, Sophie, and you have school tomorrow." Brenda frowned as the knock came again. "Charlie! Charlie, can you please get that? I'm helping Sophie."

"I don't want to go to school." Sophie wailed and collapsed onto the floor.

"Sophie." Brenda sighed and tried to be patient. The weekend had been chaotic, and she was out of her routine. "Let's go, I'll read you an extra book tonight." She helped her daughter to her feet and looked into her big, sad eyes.

"But I don't want to go to bed!" Sophie wailed again.

Someone pounded on the door.

"Charlie!" Brenda felt herself tip over the edge of frustration. She wrapped her daughter in a towel, carried her into her room, then set her on her bed. "Please get your pajamas on, okay?"

"Fine." Sophie stomped over to her dresser.

As another round of knocks were delivered against the door, Brenda thought she might just lose her mind. She saw Charlie's office door was still shut. She knew he could hear her. Fed up, she marched to the door and threw it open.

"Yes?" Her sharp tone faded as she recognized Detective Crackle. "Detective, what is it?"

"Hi Brenda." His gaze passed over her shirt and jeans which were splashed with water from Sophie's bath. "I hope this isn't a bad time."

"It is." Brenda frowned as she stared at him. "Did something happen? Did you find Alexa's killer?"

"No, I'm sorry to say. Actually, I'm here to speak with Charlie. Is he available?" He stepped into the house, despite the fact that he hadn't been invited inside.

"Charlie?" Brenda shook her head. "He's in the middle of an article and—"

"It's important." He crossed his arms as he studied her. "I wouldn't be here at this hour if it wasn't."

"It's important that you need to talk to Charlie?" Brenda stared back at him as she attempted to comprehend why he would need to speak to her husband. "What is this about?"

"Mommy!" Sophie screeched as she padded out into the hallway.

Brenda spun around to see her daughter with her pajama top tangled around her head and shoulders.

"Help! I'm stuck! Help!"

"Oh dear." Detective Crackle tried to cover a chuckle with a cough.

"Oh Sophie." Brenda had to hide her own smile as she hurried over to help her daughter. When she passed Charlie's office she banged on the door. "Charlie, I need you out here."

"What is it?" Charlie threw open the door, his cheeks flushed and his eyes sharp. "I am on a deadline, I told you that!" He froze as he caught sight of

Detective Crackle in the living room. "What's going on here?"

Brenda sighed as she looked at her husband. Charlie was usually patient, and kind, and supportive. But when he had a deadline, he could lose his temper from the pressure he was under.

"I'm sorry, I know. Detective Crackle needs to speak with you, he said it's important." Brenda ushered Sophie back into her room, but lingered near the door so that she could hear the conversation outside.

"Detective Crackle, I'm really under the gun here, I hate to rush you but can whatever it is wait?"

"No, it can't, I'm sorry. I wasn't aware that you had a connection to Alexa. I need you to tell me your history with her."

"History? There isn't one. She worked at the newspaper a couple of years ago, that was it."

"There was never anything of a personal nature between the two of you?"

"What? No, of course not."

"It's important that you tell me the truth, Charlie. I need to know if you and Alexa ever discussed any issues she had, with a boyfriend, with family, with friends?"

"No. Nothing like that. I asked her how she

dealt with the fame she got from her vlogs, and she said she had a friend back home that kept her down to earth. That was all."

"And who was this friend?"

Brenda closed her eyes as she realized that Joyce must have passed the information she had given her to Detective Crackle. She could understand why, but she knew that Charlie would be frustrated about it. Detective Crackle couldn't really consider Charlie a suspect, could he?

"Her name is Poppy. I remember because I thought it was kind of an odd name. Anyway, she said this friend was always there for her, and reminded her where she came from, so that her ego didn't get too inflated. But if you ask me, it was still pretty big. She had a lot of demands, and not a lot of patience."

"That's an easy way to make some enemies. So, did you see her while she was in town?"

"No, I didn't. I haven't spoken to her in years."

"You're not lying to me are you, Charlie?"

Brenda's eyes widened at the question and the tone in which it was delivered. Annoyed, she opened Sophie's door and stepped back out into the living room.

"Did you get what you needed, Detective?"

Brenda paused beside Charlie and stared at the detective.

"Charlie and I were just finishing up." He kept his gaze fixed on Charlie, despite answering her.

"No, we are finished. If you think you need to question me further about this, then you'd better invite me down to the station." Charlie shook his head. "I have nothing to hide."

"Charlie." Brenda placed her hand lightly on his shoulder. "He's just doing his job."

"Sure, and I'm just trying to do mine." Charlie glanced once more in Detective Crackle's direction, then headed back to his office. "Please, no more interruptions."

"I'll do my best, Charlie." Brenda sighed as she walked the detective to the door. "I'm sorry, when he's on a deadline he gets really worked up."

"Are you sure that's all it's about?" Detective Crackle raised an eyebrow. "Maybe he's tense about Alexa's murder?"

"Detective, I don't know what you're digging for, but you're certainly not going to find anything here."

"Like you said, Brenda, I'm just doing my job. With Alexa being so involved in the media, there are many suspects for me to wade through. I need to be sure that I'm being thorough, and certainly not showing any favoritism." Detective Crackle lowered his eyes, then looked back at her. "You understand that, don't you?"

"I guess, but you're wasting your time on this. Charlie didn't know Alexa really. Your focus needs to be on the real suspects. I spoke to Kevin earlier, and he seemed pretty upset that Alexa and one of the other protesters had instigated the chaos during the protest. Maybe you should track down that other protestor, from the video I saw my guess is it was Mark." She held the door open for him. "Charlie has nothing to do with any of this."

"You can trust that I am investigating all avenues of the case. I have to explore all avenues, sometimes people know things without realizing they know them. In my experience the most important clue can be found in the most unexpected places." He tipped his hat to her. "Thanks for your time, Brenda, and I do apologize for invading your evening."

"Good night, Detective." Brenda's heart softened some as she watched him walk away. Yes, it annoyed her that he had demanded to speak to Charlie, but he did seem very dedicated to solving the murder.

Joyce settled at the kitchen table with her computer and began to dig into Alexa's social media. So far all she had was a first name for Poppy, but if they had been friends for as long as it seemed, she guessed that there would be plenty of pictures online of them together. After some searching, she did find some pictures, but none with Poppy's name listed. She noticed that Poppy tended to turn her face away from the camera, and though she was often by Alexa's side, she rarely looked in the same direction.

Mark was also featured in many photographs, with his name listed. However, he didn't seem to show any animosity towards either woman in the pictures. In fact, he often had his arm hooked through Alexa's, or gazed at her with admiration as the photo was snapped. That was a far different attitude than he had presented when he spoke about Alexa at the coffee shop. Joyce rubbed a hand across her eyes as she tried to concentrate. The more she looked into Alexa, the more apprehensive she became about Vanessa. What if they were wrong? What if Vanessa really did have something to do with it?

Joyce took a deep breath, then switched her

search to Vanessa. Even though she didn't know the woman very well, she felt a bit guilty for stalking her. But she still couldn't believe that she would make a deal with *Country Grocery Place*, like Detective Crackle had said, and hoped to find some proof that it wasn't true. However, it didn't take long for her to find something that made her heart drop. There was a photograph of Vanessa at a grand opening of *Country Grocery Place*. She was standing next to the man cutting the ribbon outside the doors. He was listed as the owner of the grocery chain. The picture was from about a month before. It was next to an article that mentioned the new product lines that the grocery store was planning on introducing, including more vegan options.

Although there weren't more details listed with it, along with what Detective Crackle had said, the article and the image itself pretty much confirmed that Vanessa struck some kind of deal with *Country Grocery Place*. That was likely the evidence that Alexa planned to reveal to her followers. Even though Detective Crackle had mentioned the deal, and the article and photo supported it, Joyce still couldn't quite believe it, she couldn't imagine Vanessa agreeing to a deal that would put her standards at risk. She was so passionate about the food she sold being safe and organic. She decided the best way to find out the whole truth was to consult the source.

With this on her mind, she decided to place a call to Vanessa. After the third ring, she heard someone pick up. However, there was a lot of noise in the background before Vanessa's voice finally came on the line.

"Hello?" The slurring of her words made Joyce wonder if Vanessa might have been sleeping, or if she was quite drunk.

"Hi Vanessa, it's Joyce. I'm sorry to bother you."

"It's no bother. What did you need?"

"I just wanted to ask you something. I found a picture of you at an opening of *Country Grocery Place* and I've heard some rumors. Do you have some kind of deal going with them?" Joyce braced herself for what the woman's reaction might be. Would she deny it, or laugh it off as not being a very big deal?

"Deal? Well, yes. I recently signed a contract with *Country Grocery Place* to sell packaged meals in all of their stores. I thought it was a pretty amazing offer."

"It sounds amazing. You were going to sell the same products you do on your truck? All vegan?"

"Vegan and organic, yes. The same stuff I sell on

my truck." Vanessa sighed. "Well, not exactly the same. I get my produce from local sources, but in order to make the meals in the mass amounts and sell them through the grocery store I had to agree to use their suppliers for the produce."

"I see. Are the suppliers organic?" Joyce narrowed her eyes as a theory began to form in her mind.

"They must be. *Country Grocery Place* knows that I advertise that only organic products are used in my meals. But honestly I don't know for sure, I just presumed they must be." Vanessa paused. Then her voice raised some. "Why? Do you know something I don't?"

"I was just curious. I didn't mean to upset you, I'm sorry." Joyce frowned as she sensed the woman was getting a bit upset.

"It's okay, Joyce. I'm sorry, too. It's just that the police asked me so many questions. Many times, the same questions over and over again. I'm just feeling so paranoid, and unsettled. I didn't mean to get upset."

"You have every right to be upset, Vanessa." Joyce softened her tone. "You've been through a lot. I want you to know, Brenda and I never thought you were involved in any of this."

"Of course, you didn't. You're good friends. I'm afraid my reputation in this town might just be ruined, though. No one is going to forget that I was a suspect."

"I wouldn't worry about that too much, Vanessa. Once they find the true killer, everyone will know that you had nothing to do with it. You would be surprised how quickly people around here move forward. It's a kind town." Joyce took a deep breath as she hoped that would turn out to be true. "Just one last thing, Vanessa. Why do you think Alexa asked you to meet her that morning?"

"She told me that she owed me an apology, and she wanted to talk to me about something. I was pretty sure it was some kind of trap, but I went to meet her, anyway. I guess I'll never know what she had to tell me." Vanessa sighed.

"Try to have a good night, Vanessa. I'm sure things will look brighter in the morning."

"I hope so," Vanessa mumbled a goodbye, then hung up the phone.

Joyce typed out a message to Brenda detailing what she had found. Now, she believed she knew how Alexa intended to expose Vanessa's deal. What she couldn't figure out was why Alexa had recorded the final video. What did she have to apologize for?

Maybe Vanessa didn't know it, but she did make a deal with the very company that Alexa had protested against. Maybe Alexa discovered that Vanessa was clueless about the pesticides and wanted to reveal the truth to her instead of ruining her reputation?

Joyce looked back at a picture of Alexa on her website. She had those black spiked cuffs around her wrists. They looked so sharp she wondered how she didn't scratch herself on occasion. Suddenly, the scratch on Mark's neck flashed back through her mind. Maybe those spikes had scratched Mark. Her stomach flipped at the thought. Mark had motive, he had opportunity, and he had a scratch on his neck. Maybe Detective Crackle was focused on Vanessa, but her attention had just shifted entirely onto Mark. The problem was Mark was nowhere to be found. But perhaps someone else knew where he was, someone who knew him well enough to shove him. Did Poppy know that Mark planned to kill her best friend?

CHAPTER 11

*J*oyce immediately shifted gears and began to hunt down Poppy. There weren't too many motels in the area, and she guessed that the woman had to be staying in one. With her bright red hair, she would be fairly easy to remember. One by one she called each of the local motels until a clerk, who was luckily a regular at the donut truck admitted that he'd seen a woman with bright red hair. After an elaborate story about how they were friends, but she had lost her number, he told her the room she was staying in.

Joyce jotted down the address for the motel, then glanced at the clock. It was nearly nine. But that could work in her favor. If Poppy was staying at the motel, then she would likely be in for the evening, or coming back soon. She decided she would stage a little stakeout of her own. For a moment she considered contacting Detective Crackle to see if he wanted to join her, but she decided against it. He had his own way of investigating, and she didn't want to be held back by it. She didn't want him to try to stop her either.

Joyce grabbed her jacket and a few snacks to stash in the car, then headed out. It wasn't that long ago that she locked the door around six and went to bed an hour or so later. After Davey died, she focused on routine to get her through her grief. Eventually, she sank into an extreme sense of boredom. It was then that she began to get a bit more creative with her time. But staking out a motel room after dark was a new kind of creativity for her. She parked far enough from the motel room to go unnoticed, but close enough to be able to see who was going in and out the door. As she turned her radio on low she thought about what Brenda's evening might be like. She hoped it had calmed down at least a little bit, but if Detective Crackle had anything to do with it, she doubted it would. The man could be so stubborn.

Joyce settled back in the driver's seat and watched the motel room through the windshield. As she broke open her first bag of chips, she wondered if she would really find out anything by being there. As if to answer the question, a car pulled up in front of her. The headlights flashed through the windshield for a few seconds before the car turned into a parking space in front of the motel room.

Joyce leaned forward, ready to see Poppy step out of the car. The lights on the outside of the motel were bright enough to illuminate the sidewalk that ran in front of each door. As a figure stepped out of the car, she peered through the glass. A second later the figure stepped into the light, and to her surprise she discovered it wasn't Poppy at all, but Mark.

Joyce's heart jumped into her throat. What was he doing there? Was he staying at the same motel? She couldn't imagine that he would be, otherwise Detective Crackle would have been able to find him easily. Whether or not he was staying there, he seemed at ease as he walked up to the door of the room where Poppy was supposed to be staying.

Joyce's heart lurched. What if he was there to go after Poppy? If he had done something to hurt Alexa, he might feel the need to harm Poppy as well.

As he reached for the door handle, she began to panic. If Mark was there to harm Poppy, then it could all happen very quickly, and she would have no way to protect herself.

There wasn't really a decision to make, she had to do whatever it took to protect Poppy. As she stepped out of her car, the door to the motel room swung open. She couldn't tell whether Mark had opened it, or Poppy had, as the woman stood in the doorway.

Joyce froze where she was. If she was spotted, neither of them showed it. They stood in the doorway for a few minutes, their voices just loud enough so Joyce was able to catch a few tidbits of their conversation.

"We can't wait any longer. We have to move forward." Mark insisted, then glanced over his shoulder.

Joyce ducked down behind her car, out of view, though she could still hear them.

"It doesn't seem like the right time." Poppy grabbed his sleeve. "Come inside."

"No, I can't stay long. I'm doing this, tomorrow. Are you ready?" He pulled back a few steps from her.

"We need to talk about this." Poppy grabbed his hand, and pulled him towards the door.

This time Mark didn't resist. Instead, he disappeared inside the motel room. When the door closed, Joyce straightened up. Her knees ached from crouching so long. But she wasn't ready to get into her car and leave. She suspected there was more to find out. What she'd overheard didn't make much sense to her. She wanted to find out what they were planning to do, and whether it had anything to do with Alexa.

As Joyce crept closer to the motel room, the very lights that had allowed her a clear view of the pair on the sidewalk, seemed to work against her. At any second, she expected to be noticed, and what explanation could she give for her presence? She had no reason to be out at the motel at that time of night. Still, she couldn't resist pressing her ear against the door. Their voices were muffled, too muffled for her to make out many words. As she continued to listen, she heard their voices become clearer.

"I'm counting on you, Poppy."

"I know, I know. Just be patient with me."

It suddenly occurred to Joyce that the reason their voices were clearer was because they were getting closer to the door. She gasped as she ducked back into a small alcove just before the door swung open. Had they heard her? She held her breath as Mark walked past, and headed back to his car. He glanced back once over his shoulder at Poppy. When she closed the door to the motel room, he pulled open his car door, and slid inside.

Joyce lingered there, even after the car pulled away. She thought for a moment about knocking on the motel room door and having a conversation with Poppy. But again, there was no good excuse for her being there, and she doubted that Poppy would be too eager to speak to a stranger.

Armed with the knowledge that there seemed to be some secrets between Poppy and Mark, Joyce got back into her car and drove back to her house. In just a few hours she would be at the truck with Brenda, and she hoped that she would be able to shed some clarity on what might be happening between Mark and Poppy. One thing she noticed, was that Poppy didn't seem all that broken up over her friend's death. Perhaps she was just putting on a brave face for Mark, or maybe she was scared of him. Did she know what happened to Alexa? The question burned through her mind as she paced the living room. If even the people closest to Alexa were up to something behind her back, then did she truly have any friends?

∽

When Brenda woke up the next morning, she smelled coffee. It was a lovely smell, until she realized that it shouldn't be wafting through her bedroom. Her alarm hadn't even gone off, yet. Had she left the pot on from the night before? She sat up in bed and reached for her husband. When she found Charlie's side of the bed empty, her focus shifted to the bedroom door. What was he doing up so early? She made her way into the kitchen and found toast just popped out of the toaster, and Charlie with the coffee pot in his hand.

"Morning, sweetheart."

"Morning." Brenda blinked. "What are you doing up?"

"Listen, I'm sorry about last night." Charlie poured coffee into a mug for her, then handed it to her. "I know I was out of sorts, and I shouldn't have snapped at you like that."

"It's okay, Charlie, I know how much pressure you were under. I should have just sent Detective

Crackle away." She took the coffee from him. "Thanks for this."

"No, it was the right thing to do, I wouldn't want to interfere with the investigation. But it never feels good when the suspicion turns on you." He grimaced.

"The best thing I can think of to do is help find out who really did this. Once this is solved you won't have to worry about it." Brenda picked up her phone and powered it on. "I'm hoping that maybe Joyce will have some ideas when I get to the truck."

"That would be good." Charlie took a sip of his coffee.

"Oh, actually I have a text from her." She read it out loud to Charlie. "So, it looks like Vanessa is almost definitely involved with *Country Grocery Place* and that would certainly cause Alexa to target her. But according to Joyce, she doesn't think that Vanessa was aware of what she was committing herself to. Maybe that's why Alexa never went through with exposing Vanessa's connection."

"Maybe." He frowned. "It sounds like some possibly dishonest practices on the part of *Country Grocery Place*. But why would that stop Alexa?"

"Let's say that Alexa figured that out. What if she was going to go after Vanessa, but then she realized that Vanessa had no idea what kind of mess she'd gotten herself into. She realized that she was about to destroy her business, and her life, and decided not to do it."

"That's quite a theory. But I'm not sure how you could prove it." Charlie set his coffee mug down and wrapped his arms around her. "I just assumed that the person who abducted her had forced her to post that video."

"I think we all assumed that. But what if the person who abducted her was really trying to stop the video? It was live, so it was being actively posted as Alexa recorded it. Maybe whoever took her wanted to silence her, and couldn't prevent being recorded in the process." Brenda tapped her fingers on her coffee mug. "But who would want to stop that video?"

"Do you think the final video was going to be an apology to Vanessa?" He leaned back against the counter.

"I think it could have been. I imagine Vanessa had already suffered some loss of business just from Alexa mentioning that she might have something to hide. Maybe Alexa wanted to set the record straight." Brenda took a sip of her coffee. "A last act of kindness."

"See, that's the part I'm not so sure about." Charlie shook his head. "Alexa never seemed like a kind person to me."

"I'd have to agree with you there. And apparently Mark wasn't fond of her. Maybe Poppy was her only true friend. She would probably be the best person to ask." Brenda glanced at her phone again. "I wonder if the police have been able to locate her."

"Well, Detective Crackle sure had no problem locating me." Charlie chuckled. "I think I owe him an apology, too."

"Really? I thought he was a bit intrusive and rude." Brenda pursed her lips.

"As he needs to be in order to solve a crime. I could have been far more accommodating. Honestly, I give him credit for not putting me in handcuffs." He blushed as he set his empty coffee mug in the sink.

"I would never let that happen." Brenda cupped his cheeks and looked into his eyes.

"Oh really? And how would you stop it?" He grinned as he gazed back at her.

"Well, I would have knocked him out of course." She smiled.

"Sure, then we could be in handcuffs together." Charlie winked at her.

"I could think of worse things." Brenda grinned as she placed a light kiss on his lips. "Thanks for the coffee. I need to get the truck moved so I have to go. I love you, Charlie."

"I love you, too." He pulled her into a warm hug. "Always."

"I know, sweetheart." She kissed his cheek. "Even when you're on a deadline."

After Brenda dressed and gave Sophie a kiss goodbye she headed out to her car. In the darkness that lingered before dawn she could see the town was still not ready to wake up. Some houses had lights on, while most were still dim and quiet. She was lulled into a comfortable sense of peace. When her cell phone rang, she nearly jumped out of her skin. She checked the phone and saw that it was Melissa. Once she reached the truck, she returned her call.

The phone rang several times before Melissa finally picked it up.

"Hi Brenda. Sorry I called so early."

"It's fine, I'm just moving the truck to the new spot." She paused as she unlocked the door. "So, what's up?"

"I just wanted to tell you, I really enjoy my job

on the truck. I know I still have a lot to learn, but I promise I will try hard."

"I know you will, Melissa. You're doing a great job." Brenda climbed into the truck and checked over everything to make sure nothing was out of place. "What's going on, hon? Are you okay?"

"I just wanted you to know that I'll be there this morning. Thanks so much for this opportunity."

"You're welcome, Melissa." Brenda frowned. "Are you sure there's nothing wrong?"

"Nothing. I'll see you soon."

Brenda hung up the phone and stared at it for a moment. She'd noticed Melissa acted strangely when the police were around. Now it seemed she was acting even more strangely. She knew that she couldn't force her to talk, she just hoped that when she was ready to express what was on her mind, she would.

Just as Brenda tucked her phone into her pocket it buzzed with a text. She pulled it out to check it. Once she saw that it was from Detective Crackle, she read it. He asked if she would have time to speak to him later that morning. She hesitated. What if he wanted to talk about Charlie? She knew she didn't have much choice since she would have to face him eventually. After the chaos he'd witnessed in her home the night before, she wondered if his opinion of her had changed. Reluctantly, she texted back that she would be available. Then she started the truck. She had a feeling it was going to be a long and strange day.

CHAPTER 12

Brenda eased the truck into park, then went through the process of setting it up. Her thoughts shifted to Charlie, and how kind he had been to her that morning. Their marriage had always been based on teamwork. They propped each other up at every turn. Although he'd been shocked and hesitant over her desire to work with Joyce on the donut truck, he'd supported her despite his misgivings. Without question she wanted to support him, but she wasn't sure how. If she told Detective Crackle exactly what she thought of his visit, then she could alienate him, and any chance of having updates about the investigation would go right out the window. Still, holding in her frustration was very difficult for her to do. When he showed up, she had no idea how she would react.

"Morning Brenda." Joyce's voice drifted up the stairs, followed by her presence.

"Joyce." Brenda turned towards her and managed a brief smile. "How are you this morning?"

"I'm more concerned about you. Are you okay?" Joyce walked over to her friend, her eyes already digging for the truth.

"I will be." She narrowed her eyes. "We had a visit from Detective Crackle last night."

"Oh, I was afraid of that." She clasped her hands together. "That might be my fault."

"It's okay, Joyce, it's not your fault. I just feel like Detective Crackle is spinning his wheels and we need to find a way to get ahead of this." She sunk her hands into the dough she had prepared and began to form a few balls into donuts.

"I might have some information to help with that, but honestly I'm not sure what to make of it." Joyce leaned back against the counter and recounted what she had seen and heard the night before. By the time she finished the first batch of donuts was in, and Brenda had a thoughtful look on her face.

"Did Poppy seem scared to you?" Brenda washed her hands off, then used a towel to dry them.

"It was hard to tell. Honestly, I didn't think she was scared. It was almost as if they were in a bit of a fight. Nothing extreme, but it seemed as if Mark wanted something from her that maybe she wasn't ready to give him." Joyce brushed a wisp of her hair away from her eyes as she recalled the conversation from the night before. "I didn't catch everything."

"I think we should consider that Poppy could still be in danger. If Mark did this, then he may be going after her to keep her quiet. If they were all friends then there is a good chance that Poppy at least suspects him, or will in time." Brenda checked the donuts, then turned around to fill the napkin dispenser. "Unfortunately, I'm not sure that sending Detective Crackle into the mix is the best way to handle this either."

"I can understand that after what happened last night." Joyce lowered her eyes as guilt twisted her stomach. "I'm really sorry about that, Brenda."

"There's nothing to be sorry about." Brenda met her friend's eyes and held them. "Detective Crackle was just doing his job, I get that. But that's the problem. He does his job, to the letter of the law, and when it comes to this situation I think there needs to be some flexibility in how we approach it."

"I agree." Joyce pursed her lips as she considered their options. "As you recall, there were several people there at the protest. Everyone claims they saw nothing incriminating, but maybe that is because they didn't understand what they saw."

"What do you mean?" Brenda lifted the donuts out of the oil and let them drain.

"I'm not sure, but I'm convinced that someone in that crowd knows something that will help explain what happened to Alexa, and is not willing to talk about it, or doesn't know it is relevant."

"Someone like me?" Melissa stepped off the last step into the truck. She glanced between the two women and offered a brief nod to each. "I realized last night that I did see something more on the day of the protest."

"But you were in the truck with us." Brenda watched her with interest.

"I was during the protest, but earlier in the day I had encountered Mark and Alexa. I saw them filming a video. Alexa was asking Mark questions about the last protest, and whether he was expecting anything to get out of hand this time. He said he wasn't, and that he was sure that despite how passionate people were about protecting their food, they could still keep cool heads and prevent destruction from happening." Melissa sighed and crossed her arms. "You know I was a huge fan of Alexa, so I hung around and listened. It felt like I was getting an exclusive vlog, I couldn't help it."

"Okay, that's understandable. But why are you bringing it up now?" Brenda tilted her head to the side and looked deeper into Melissa's eyes. "Was there something else you overheard?"

"When Alexa turned the camera off, Mark suggested they get more film of Vanessa's truck and her customers. Maybe even try to get some video testimonies from some of the customers." Melissa bit into her bottom lip, then frowned. "I just didn't think it had anything to do with the murder. But ever since Vanessa was taken in for questioning, I've wondered if maybe she caught them filming and figured out what they were planning."

"So, you think they wanted the video to further embarrass her?" Joyce raised an eyebrow. "Are you sure about that?"

"The way they were talking about it, yes, I'm

sure about it. They wanted to create a big scandal." Melissa frowned. "It made me so uncomfortable. It's just not the type of person that I thought Alexa was."

"And you never mentioned any of this to the police?" Brenda crossed her arms.

"No, I just didn't think it was important. I think that the final video she filmed had to do with Vanessa," Melissa said.

"I agree." Brenda nodded. "I think she was probably going to apologize to her, because she found out Vanessa didn't have a clue what *Country Grocery Place* is up to. Vanessa presumed that the ingredients she would have to use would adhere to her current philosophy. That the products were going to be organic and vegan. She trusted them. She was naïve. She's just a regular business owner who is trying to survive."

"I suppose it's possible Alexa's convictions didn't extend further than the camera lens." Joyce shook her head. "I'm not so sure she was actually preparing to apologize. She might have just been setting Vanessa up."

"That's what I thought, too." Melissa nodded.

"Do you have the picture you found last night,

the one taken outside *Country Grocery Place*?" Brenda looked at Joyce.

"Yes." Joyce pulled out her phone and showed it to Brenda.

"That's the owner?" Brenda's eyes widened as she looked at the tall man with broad shoulders.

"Yes, from what I can tell." Joyce nodded.

"I think I've seen him before, but I can't be sure." Brenda looked closer at the picture. "In the parking lot, the morning Alexa was murdered. He looked so relaxed in all of the chaos."

"Really?" Joyce's heart raced. "Maybe he paid someone to take Alexa out and he was there to see the proof and give himself an alibi. You better call the detective and let him know. This could change everything."

"I will. He is coming in to see me this morning, but I'll call him first." Brenda nodded. "I'm not sure it's him though, but any little bit of information could lead to a lot more."

"Speaking of which, I'm going to have a conversation with Poppy. Once and for all, I want to hear her side of all of this. If she is in danger, she needs to be warned. Even if Mark isn't the murderer, he seems to be the center of all of this, and we know that he's the one who took down the videos on Alexa's vlog." Joyce picked up her purse. "You don't mind do you, Brenda?"

"No, I don't mind, but I don't think you should go by yourself." She glanced over at Melissa, then back at Joyce. "Why don't you just wait until after we close down for the day."

"I can't, Brenda. At this point we believe that Kevin wasn't involved, and neither of us really think that Vanessa had anything to do with it. The owner is someone to look into. But I am worried about Mark, and if he was involved I don't think we have time to waste. I saw him at the motel. He knows where she's staying, and if she begins to suspect him, then he might do something to hurt her. Brenda, I will never be able to forgive myself if I don't go make sure that Poppy is okay."

"I understand." Brenda placed her hands on her shoulders. "If you just wait until after morning rush, I'll go with you."

"I can't." Joyce narrowed her eyes. "I'm sorry, Brenda, but my instincts are telling me I need to go now. Please, don't try any of that overprotective nonsense with me right now. I'm going, and I'll be perfectly fine on my own." She started down the steps of the truck.

"Joyce!" Brenda frowned as she followed after her. "Just be sure to keep your distance, all right? If Mark is there, make sure you are careful. Call me and let me know what is going on. Okay?"

"I will." Joyce glanced back up at her as she stepped off the truck. "I'll be fine, Brenda. I promise."

Brenda watched her walk away, and wanted to believe her final words, but her own instincts told her something very different.

∽

To Brenda's relief Detective Crackle didn't answer his phone, she wasn't in the mood to speak to him after last night and she hoped that he didn't come to speak to her like he said he would. She left a message about the possibility that the owner of *Country Grocery Place* was in the parking lot when Alexa's body was dumped. Shortly after she hung up there was a rush of customers. Despite being distracted by her concern for Joyce, Brenda managed to keep up with serving the customers. When she saw one in particular approach the truck, her heart skipped a beat. She stared at him for a second to be sure he was who she thought he was.

Mark paused in front of the window and stared back at her.

"Can I get a couple of original glazed please?" Mark nodded. "I only eat organic, but I promised these to a friend."

"Sure." Brenda looked at Melissa.

Melissa nodded slightly, her gaze lingered on Mark as well.

"Thanks." Mark looked over his shoulder, then back at them. "I'm in a hurry."

"Here you go." Brenda handed him the box.

"Oh wait, I remember you." He smiled as he met Brenda's eyes. "Where's your friend?"

"She's not here right now." Brenda cleared her throat. "She's going to be sorry that she missed you."

"I bet." Mark quirked an eyebrow. "Maybe I'll do a review on your truck. Would you like that?"

"Of course." Brenda's heart fluttered as she didn't know what else to say. "That would be great."

"I'll try to get it done before I leave today. But right now I have to run." He tipped his head to her, then walked off.

It wasn't until he left that she realized that she hadn't charged him. Did she just hand over free donuts to the person that killed Alexa?

"That was strange." Melissa stood beside her with her arms crossed. "What was he talking about?"

"It's a long story." Brenda sighed as she watched him disappear into the crowd. If he was leaving, there was very little time left to prove that he was involved in Alexa's death. She pulled out her phone to send a text to Joyce. There was still a chance that he would go after Poppy before he left. However, before she could type anything out, someone knocked on the counter in front of her. She jumped at the sound and looked up into Detective Crackle's eyes.

"Are you free?"

Brenda's throat went dry as she thought of all of the reasons she should avoid a conversation with him. Then she reminded herself that he was the best chance they had of getting the murder solved.

"Sure, Detective. Melissa, I'm going to step out for just a minute." Brenda glanced over at her. "I'll be right outside if you need anything."

"Okay." Melissa avoided looking directly at the detective.

Brenda pretended not to notice, but she still wondered why Melissa was so nervous around Detective Crackle. Perhaps it was because of his intimidating nature, or that she simply didn't know him very well. Either way, it wasn't what she needed to focus on at the moment.

When Brenda stepped off the truck Detective Crackle greeted her at the door.

"Thanks for taking some time out." He gestured for her to walk beside him.

"I don't want to get too far from the truck. Melissa can handle it I'm sure, but it's better to be cautious." She frowned.

"I got your message. You were right the owner of *Country Grocery Place* was at the parking lot the day of the murder. We interviewed him on the day and he claimed that he had a meeting with the owner of the sushi truck. We are still trying to confirm it." Detective Crackle slid his hands into his pockets. "I also have an update to give you on the case."

"What's the update?"

"We've ruled Kevin out as a suspect. It turns out he did have an alibi for that morning he just didn't want to share it. He arrived at the town square, just before the body was dumped." Detective Crackle sighed. "It is also looking less likely that Vanessa was involved. Although she doesn't have an alibi and she could have got someone else to dump the body, the text on her phone from Alexa asking her to meet up early that morning does appear to be genuine. Also, we found some notes on Alexa's computer that indicate she intended to protect Vanessa rather than expose her."

"That gives Vanessa a lot less motive." Brenda narrowed her eyes. "Unless she assumed that Alexa still planned to attack her."

"Yes, that possibility is still there. My instincts are telling me that she didn't harm Alexa, though. I must rely on the evidence, but I'm having a difficult time envisioning her as a murderer." Detective Crackle lowered his head and kicked the toe of his shoe against the pavement. "Listen, Brenda, I want you to know that Charlie isn't a suspect, either. I realize I could have handled that situation more delicately. I'm sorry for invading your home in that way." He glanced up at her.

"Don't worry about it." Brenda swallowed hard to hide her true feelings about the situation. "I'm sorry you had to see us on such a rough night."

"Where's Joyce?" Detective Crackle looked back at the truck. "I noticed she wasn't inside."

"Oh, she went off for a bit." Brenda almost told

him where, then hesitated. She wanted to give Joyce a chance to talk with Poppy, and if Detective Crackle interrupted that conversation, she might not be as forthcoming. "Listen Detective, Mark was just here. My instincts are telling me he's involved in all of this. He deleted the videos, he was in a bit of a feud with Alexa, and he doesn't seem like the type to want to share the limelight."

"I don't disagree with you. However, the evidence hasn't lined up just yet." Detective Crackle ran a hand along his chin, then sighed. "He's a slippery fellow."

"He's about to get even more slippery." Brenda met his eyes. "He said that he was leaving today."

"That's not good." He gritted his teeth. "I'd better get my hands on him before he takes off. I do want to find out more about his relationship with Alexa."

"I hope you can find him." Brenda shivered. "I just wish all of this was over."

"Me, too." Detective Crackle pulled off his hat, waved it in front of his face to swat away a fly, then set it back on his head. "To be honest with you, Brenda, I'm not sure that we will solve this. There simply isn't enough evidence."

"What about the car? Did you ever find it?"

STRAWBERRY DONUTS AND SCANDAL

Brenda's stomach clenched at the memory of seeing that car pulling away.

"No. I placed a call to all of the local auto shops. I thought if the taillights weren't working on the car, maybe someone took it in for repair. I didn't find the car, I'm going to try the car rental places next. It's a long shot, but hopefully it will lead to something."

"Good luck, Detective. I hope that you find something." Brenda started back towards the truck.

"Thank you!" He called out to her. "Oh, and when you see Joyce, please ask her to call me. There's something I need to discuss with her."

"Sure, I will." Brenda nodded to him, then headed up the steps into the truck. She stepped inside just as a cloud of smoke drifted out. As she coughed and waved her hand through it, she heard a commotion farther inside the truck. "Melissa?"

"I'm so sorry!" She gasped as she tossed a pile of very burnt donuts into the sink. "There were no flames, I swear."

"What happened?" Brenda coughed again and flipped on the fan to blow some of the smoke out of the truck.

"I got distracted. I'm so sorry, Brenda. I didn't mean to." Melissa grabbed a piece of paper to fan the smoke.

"It's okay." Brenda smiled as she touched her shoulder. "We've all burnt a few donuts."

Although she hoped to reassure the young woman, she noticed her fearful expression. With no one lined up at the truck, she couldn't help but wonder what might have distracted her.

CHAPTER 13

*J*oyce drove towards the motel with a bit of a chip on her shoulder. She couldn't help being annoyed with Brenda. She loved her friend, but she didn't like to be treated as if she was incapable of anything. The best way to remind her of just how capable she was, was to solve this crime. She parked in the second row of spaces, then climbed out of the car. As she approached the motel room she didn't see any sign of Mark's car. That gave her some relief. However, that relief was short-lived.

Joyce paused outside the motel room door, and winced. Inside she could hear arguing. Two voices raised, and the anger was getting more intense by the second. She tensed up, even though the voice was muffled by the door the volume of it meant she could recognize it as Mark's voice. She decided to try to get a closer look. The front window of the motel room had a curtain pulled over it. She tried to peer through the edge of it, but it looked as if it had been taped down along the edges. It was the only window. With no ability to see inside, she lingered near the front door. As she leaned close, she tried to pick up on a few words in their conversation.

"Joyce? Joyce! What are you doing here?" The cheerful voice sent chills down Joyce's spine as she looked up to see a familiar face headed in her direction.

"Oh hi, Sarah. I was just leaving, actually." Joyce stepped away from the door. Hopefully, the two people inside were too busy arguing to hear the conversation outside, otherwise her cover was blown.

"Oh, where to?" Sarah followed Joyce away from the door of the motel room.

"I had a friend coming into town to stay here, but it turns out she didn't make it." Joyce frowned. "I'm not sure what happened, but apparently somehow she missed her flight."

"Sorry to hear that." Sarah frowned. "I know that you are always working on that truck, it's nice to see you taking a break. You know, Joyce, at our age, we should be resting more, not working around the clock."

"Yes, I suppose you're right, Sarah." Joyce bit the tip of her tongue to keep from pointing out that there was no particular age when people were expected to turn in a normal life for one of sedentary boredom. Sarah was only a year older than her, but she played up her role as a grandmother, as indicated by the sweater she wore. It featured the words, 'World's Best Grandma'. "I'm so sorry that I can't chat more, but I really should be on my way." She started towards her car.

"Oh, I understand." Sarah waved her hand. "I was just dropping off a flier for the bake sale next week. You and Brenda will donate some donuts, right?"

"Absolutely. You can send me a text with the kinds you would like." Joyce glanced past her to the motel room. As far as she could tell no one had come out, but with Sarah distracting her she couldn't be sure. Was Poppy okay in there alone with Mark?

"Sure, I'll do that. Okay, see you later, Joyce." Sarah waved as she walked off to her car.

Joyce ached to go back to the motel room and check on Poppy, but she felt Sarah's eyes on her.

Reluctantly, she climbed into her car and started it. Unfortunately, Sarah didn't pull out as she'd hoped. Instead, she seemed to be waiting to see if Joyce would leave. Frustrated, but eager to get back to a little sleuthing, Joyce pulled out of the parking lot and drove around the block. When she returned, Sarah's car was gone. She parked again. As she approached the door she had no idea what might have happened while she was gone. Luckily, she didn't hear arguing. Perhaps they had left, and she would have a chance to have a look in the motel room. As she paused just outside the door, she noticed that she might have a good chance at that. The door wasn't quite closed. She took a deep breath. Maybe the pair had realized she was outside and left in a hurry.

Joyce pushed the door open, hoping that the silence meant that they had both left. In the darkness beyond the door, she couldn't tell for certain if there was anyone else there. Still, she froze after taking just a few steps inside. Though she couldn't pinpoint why or from where, she sensed someone else's eyes on her. It was too late to turn back.

"Hello?" She took another step forward, despite her better judgment.

"I'm here." The voice drifted from the corner of

the room, and sounded strained, as if the speaker might be hurt.

"Poppy?" Joyce's heart began to pound as she fumbled on the wall for the light switch. Her fingertips bumped into the switch. She pushed it upward and anticipated the room flooded in light. Instead the darkness remained.

"Help." Poppy's voice drifted from the corner again, and sounded even weaker. "Please."

"I'm coming." Joyce reached into her purse for her phone as she approached the corner. She just had her hand around it when she caught sight of Poppy huddled, with her arms around her knees and her head down. She looked absolutely tiny. Her bright red hair curtained her face as she looked up at Joyce.

"I can't get up. I've been hurt, something's wrong with me."

"It's okay, honey. I'll help you." Joyce hit the emergency button on her phone, but left it in her purse as she reached down to help Poppy to her feet.

The moment Joyce reached down, Poppy lunged forward, and tackled her to the floor.

"Stop! What are you doing?" Joyce gasped as she tried to squirm out from under Poppy. Despite being tiny, much smaller than Joyce, she was actually quite strong. She ripped the sheet off the bed beside her and used it to wrap around Joyce's flailing arms. Within moments Joyce's arms were pinned behind her back. "Help!" Joyce shouted, just before Poppy's hand clamped over her mouth.

"Sh. You don't want to bring any unwanted attention in here." Poppy tightened the sheet. "If you scream I'm going to have to hurt you, and I don't want to hurt you. Can you be quiet?"

Joyce nodded as tears of panic flooded her eyes.

"Good." Poppy eased her hand off Joyce's mouth. "Now, I'm sorry about this. I have a grandmother, it's not like I'm a monster, but I've seen you snooping around and asking questions, and you have gotten yourself into something you shouldn't have. So, we're going to have to figure out what to do about this together."

Poppy sighed as she stood up and wiped her hands along the back of her jeans.

Joyce tilted her head to the side and noticed that there didn't appear to be anything physically wrong with Poppy. She had conned her into coming closer.

"What do I do with you?" Poppy began to pace back and forth, her figure just a shadow in the darkness.

Joyce's mind swirled with panic. Where was Mark?

"You don't have to do this, Poppy. Whatever Mark's made you do, I can help you." Joyce attempted to meet the young woman's eyes.

"Quiet!" Poppy snapped at her. "Mark has nothing to do with any of this. I am so sick of everyone else getting credit for things I do!"

"Things you do?" Joyce's throat grew dry as she realized her terrible mistake. It wasn't Mark who killed Alexa, it was Poppy.

"I'm the one that does the research, I'm the one that plans the protests, me, it's always me!" Poppy shrieked and pulled at her own hair. "I am the one that wants to protect us all, and nobody ever sees that!"

Joyce's heart raced as Poppy continued to rant. She realized that Poppy wasn't in a healthy mental state. She was unpredictable, and Joyce had no idea what might happen next.

∽

Brenda peered out through the window of the truck. Then she glanced at the clock on the wall again. Joyce should have been back already. Again, she

CINDY BELL

regretted letting her go off on her own. She insisted that she was more than capable of taking care of herself, and Brenda knew that she was. The problem was not her physical body, or mental capabilities, it was her determination and risk-taking that made Brenda worry when she was involved in something potentially dangerous. She decided to give her a call just to get an update on where she was. Instead of ringing, she heard a busy signal. In all the time she'd known Joyce she'd never gotten a busy signal on her phone. Either she answered, or it went to voicemail. With her stomach in knots she glanced over at Melissa.

"Do you think you can handle the truck by yourself for a little while?"

"Sure!" Melissa's eyes widened. "I can do it, Brenda, I promise."

"I know you can." Brenda frowned as she grabbed her light jacket. "Give me a call if Joyce gets back, all right?"

"Yes, I will. Is everything okay?" Melissa watched as Brenda tucked her phone back into her purse.

"I'm not sure. Most likely everything is fine." Brenda pointed to the next batch of donuts. "Make sure you take those out as soon as the timer goes off, all right?"

"I will." Melissa nodded.

Brenda hesitated at the top of the steps. It was quite likely that she was overreacting, and she wasn't completely confident that Melissa was ready to run the truck on her own, but she couldn't shake the feeling that something was wrong. As she descended the steps, she pulled out her phone to try Joyce's number again, but before she could dial, her cell phone began to ring. She was relieved at first as she expected it to be Joyce, but when she looked at the name on the screen, she saw that it was Detective Crackle. She almost dismissed the call as she was more concerned with where Joyce was than what he might have to say. But at the last second, she picked it up.

"Hi Detective."

"Brenda, are you with Joyce?" He sounded breathless.

"No, I'm not. I was just about to go look for her. Why?"

"She made an emergency call a few minutes ago, but there was no audio. The operator hasn't been able to get back through to her. Do you know where she was last?" The urgency in his tone made her heart beat even faster.

"Oh no, oh no, what's happened?" Brenda's mind spun. "The motel! She went to the motel to see Poppy. She thought that maybe if she talked to her, she might be able to find something out."

"She went alone?"

"Yes." Brenda winced. "I tried to talk her out of it, but—"

"I'm heading there now."

"I'll meet you there." Brenda ended the call, and tried calling Joyce's phone again. This time the call went straight to voicemail. A wave of panic washed over her. Joyce wouldn't have made an emergency call unless there was an emergency. If she was unreachable that meant something terrible must have happened. She hurried to her car and drove straight towards the motel. The entire time she wondered what she could have done to stop Joyce from going off on her own. She was so determined to get to the truth that she had been willing to risk everything, and Brenda felt as if she should have known that, and stopped her. When she caught sight of Joyce's car in the motel parking lot, her heart dropped. Why would she be parked there and not answering her phone?

STRAWBERRY DONUTS AND SCANDAL

She pulled up behind it, just as Detective Crackle's car sailed into the parking lot from the other side. He stopped right in front of the car and jumped out.

"Is she in there?" His eyes were wide with fear as he lunged towards the car.

"I don't think so." Brenda tried the doors, but they were locked. She peered through the windows. "Her purse isn't here either, and no phone."

"We need to get inside to get the trunk open." The detective walked around to the back of the car and rapped lightly on the trunk. "Joyce?"

"She's not in there! She can't be in there!" Brenda held back tears as she searched through her purse for Joyce's spare key. She had given it to her a few months before when she'd borrowed her car. She'd never got around to giving it back. "Here!" Her hand trembled as she handed it over to Detective Crackle.

He slid the key into the trunk and lifted it.

Brenda held her breath as she peered around him at the inside of the trunk.

"Nothing." For a moment Brenda was relieved, but that moment passed. Joyce was still missing. "The motel room, maybe she's in there." She started to cross the parking lot towards the door.

"Brenda, wait." He caught her by the elbow. "You should stay here. I'll take a look."

"No." She pulled her arm free of his grasp. "Not a chance, Detective. Try to keep up." Brenda's eyes flashed as they locked to his, then she turned and ran towards the motel room.

Detective Crackle mumbled something under his breath then chased after her. Once she reached the door she tried the knob, and found it was unlocked. She held her breath as she started to push the door open. Detective Crackle shoved her away from the door, pulled out his gun, and peeked through the opening. He then nudged the door the rest of the way open. He flattened himself against the wall as he stepped inside.

Brenda reached for the light switch. After flipping it off and on again she realized that it didn't work.

Detective Crackle pulled out a small flashlight and lined it up with his weapon. As the light spilled across the interior of the motel room Brenda followed its path. She saw that the sheet was torn off the bed. One of the lamps was knocked over, but had not broken. It appeared that there had been some kind of struggle. But there was no sign of anyone in the room. Detective Crackle put his finger to his lips, then pointed to the bathroom.

Brenda nodded as her chin quivered. What if Joyce was hurt? Or worse? She couldn't imagine her life without the woman who had become one of her closest friends.

Detective Crackle pushed open the bathroom door, and ducked inside with his gun pointed ahead of him. A second later he stepped back out and shook his head.

"She's not here, Brenda, I'm sorry, but she's not here."

"Then where?" Brenda gasped as she realized that not finding Joyce was almost as terrible as finding her hurt would have been. "Someone must have taken her."

"Don't touch anything. I've got the crime scene team on the way. Maybe they'll find something that will point us in the right direction." Detective Crackle stood in the middle of the room, his flashlight still on. His voice shook as he spoke. "We'll find her, Brenda, don't worry, we'll find her."

"Can't you track her cell phone or something?"

"I have someone working on that, too." Detective Crackle frowned. "Unfortunately, until we can confirm that Joyce was abducted, our resources are limited."

"I don't want to hear about limited resources! I want to know where she is! Where is she, Detective?" Brenda gasped out her words as panic threatened to overwhelm her.

"I don't know." Detective Crackle grimaced as his hands balled into fists. "I don't know, but I'm going to find her!"

CHAPTER 14

"Where are we going?" Joyce looked over at the woman in the driver's seat. Her red hair fell forward to hide her eyes, but she could see from the way she gripped the steering wheel that Poppy was stressed out.

"Quiet," Poppy snapped. It was just about the only thing she'd said to Joyce since they'd left the motel. She'd warned Joyce that if she shouted or attempted to run, she would make sure that she suffered the consequences. She even promised that if Joyce were somehow to escape, she would head straight for the food truck and make sure that Brenda never went home that night.

Joyce had no reason to doubt her threats. From what she understood, she had murdered her friend.

Not just any friend, but her best friend, whom she had known for years. If she could murder someone so close to her, what would stop her from doing the same to Joyce, or to Brenda? The thought terrified her.

"Please, maybe I can help you figure all of this out. I know you didn't plan for this." Joyce did her best to keep her voice soothing. She remembered a lesson her husband had taught her about how to act if she was ever abducted. It was best to be kind, to make the abductor like you. He encouraged her to share personal information. "You know, I have a bunny at home. Her name is Molly, and if I don't go home to her—"

"Quiet!" Poppy slammed on the brakes as she suddenly pulled into a parking lot. "I don't want to hear about your bunny, or what you think you can do to help me. My plan is not going to change just because you stuck your nose in it." She looked straight into Joyce's eyes. "You're a problem, and I am great at solving problems."

Joyce trembled as she noticed the coldness in the woman's eyes. She'd never seen such emptiness before. All of a sudden, she understood that Poppy knew exactly what she would do with her, and her plan did not involve Joyce making it out alive.

Terrified, she glanced around at her surroundings for any hint of something that could help her. She realized they were in the parking lot of the new *Country Grocery Place*. Bright ribbons and balloons hung everywhere to announce the grand opening.

"This is about Vanessa, isn't it?" Joyce forced the words past her lips.

"Of course it is. That criminal. She claims to sell organic, healthy foods, but she is going to get her produce from a poison-infested farm and sell them through a business that supports spreading poison into all of our homes. I gave all of that information to Alexa. She was supposed to expose Vanessa for who she really is, but no. She didn't do it." Poppy slammed her hand against the steering wheel. "She had no right! I'm the one that started the vlog, I'm the one that gave her all of the stories to run on it. I didn't want all of the distraction of the limelight, so I asked Alexa to be the face. When she refused to expose Vanessa, I gave her one last chance to do it, but she wouldn't. She said that the truth was being hidden from Vanessa, it wasn't her fault that she was being lied to and she wanted to apologize. But I knew the truth had to come out. That was when I knew that Alexa had become part of the problem. She would rather see our families poisoned than take a stand against a liar and a criminal." Poppy crossed her arms as she leaned back against her seat. "No guts. She didn't even stick to only eating organic food. She was never anything but a pretty face. I shouldn't have let her take all of the credit for everything I did."

"That must have upset you so much." Joyce looked towards the grocery store. She had no idea what Poppy's plan was, but she knew that as long as she kept her talking, she was distracted. As she slid her hand into her pocket she realized she only had one mint wrapper left. She had no idea whether Brenda was even looking for her, or if she was if she would find the wrappers. But it was the only thing she could think to do to leave a trail. Only Brenda would be able to find it. She closed her eyes for just a moment and wished her friend was there beside her. She was clever enough to figure out how to get out of situations like this.

"It didn't at first. I wanted her to be my face. I thought eventually she would commit to only eating organic and vegan food, she said she would and I believed her. I thought she would take a stand. But then she started twisting things. She made it all about money and appearances. Mark tried to tell me, he warned me that Alexa had gone off the rails, but I wouldn't listen. It wasn't until she pulled out on doing the exposé on Vanessa that I realized he was right. She wouldn't follow through." Her eyes widened as she stared off into space. "She was my soul mate, you know."

"I can only imagine how close you were." Joyce clasped her hands together to hide the tremble in them.

"So close." Poppy closed her eyes and a few tears slipped past. "I just wanted her to see how wrong she was. I wanted her to know that she couldn't play favorites. She liked Vanessa, that was the problem. She didn't want to ruin her life, she didn't think it was fair. Is it fair to eat toxic food? Is it fair to stand back and let these CEO criminals poison our children with no consequences?" She opened her eyes again and looked at Joyce. "Is it?"

"No." Joyce breathed. "It's not fair."

"It wasn't fair that I had to kill my best friend. It wasn't fair at all. But I had to do it for the good of all. I couldn't be selfish about it. I wanted to be, I wanted to just let her go. But then I realized how weak I was, how I was willing to let people be poisoned if it meant I got to keep Alexa at my side. That's when I knew, I had to kill her, I had to prove that I really wanted to protect the people." Poppy wiped at her cheeks. "And now, we need to make sure that this company will never forget the sacrifice that I made. It's time to send a message that will ruin this company, that will ruin the farm." She looked over at Joyce as a small smile drifted across her lips. "You can take comfort in knowing that you will be a big part of this, Joyce. Because of you, people will be protected."

Joyce nodded a little, but panic rushed through her. She was certain that her part in all of this was not one she would survive.

Brenda paced back and forth as the crime scene technicians entered the motel room.

"We can't just stand here. We have to find her!" She frowned as Detective Crackle hung up his phone.

"I'm doing everything I can, Brenda. But we have no idea where to look. I've got every car on the streets looking for Mark, and we're checking every place he's stayed or visited since he's been here. Hopefully, the search of the motel room will turn up some kind of clue."

"A clue." Brenda bit into her bottom lip. If she

knew anything about Joyce it was that she was a hound for mysteries. "If someone took her, she would have tried to leave a clue behind." She began to walk the length of the sidewalk. "But maybe not inside. She might have left something out here."

"We checked her car already and there was nothing in there." Detective Crackle followed after her.

"There's something, trust me." Brenda frowned as she scoured the sidewalk and the parking lot just beyond it. "Here!" She crouched down and picked up a small, green wrapper.

"Brenda, the parking lot is full of garbage."

"No, this is a wrapper from one of Joyce's favorite mints. She always has some on her. It might not be hers, but if it is she doesn't litter. She might have dropped it on the ground and if she did, she did so for a reason." Brenda skimmed the cars that lined the parking spaces. "Someone brought her out here. Probably to put her inside of a car." She began to walk again, towards the adjacent parking spaces. "Look!" She gasped as she headed towards another green wrapper. She paused in the middle of the parking lot and assessed the location of the wrapper. "She was put in the passenger side of a car that was parked here. See?" She pointed to the wrapper and where she stood. "That's the position the car would be in. Maybe we could check the surveillance video and see what car it was?"

"We could, but unfortunately there aren't cameras here. I already checked. I will investigate it further." Detective Crackle shoved his hands into his pockets. "The good thing is that now we know she was okay when she left here, and her abductor put her in the front seat which is a good sign."

"A good sign." Brenda nodded, then wrung her hands. "I want only good signs."

"I've got something." Detective Crackle pulled his phone out and checked it. "They've traced her phone. She's at *Country Grocery Place*." He looked up from his phone, his brows knitted with confusion. "Why would she be at a grocery store?"

"*Country Grocery Place*?" Brenda snapped her fingers. "That's the grocery store that Vanessa made a deal with to sell her products through. Plus, Alexa and Mark staged protests against them. That's more evidence that Mark was here."

"Or it could be evidence that she doesn't realize we're looking for her and she is just doing some grocery shopping." Detective Crackle tucked his phone into his pocket. "I'd prefer that myself."

"No, you saw the signs of a struggle in that

motel room, Detective. You and I both know that this was no shopping trip." Brenda started towards her car. "I'm heading there right now."

"Wait!" Detective Crackle stepped in front of her.

"Don't try to stop me!" Brenda stared into his eyes. "I never should have let her leave this morning, and nothing is going to stop me from finding her now."

"I'm not going to stop you." Detective Crackle gestured to his car. "I'm going to give you a ride. With lights and everything." He lifted his eyebrows. "Deal?"

"Deal!" Brenda followed him to his car and climbed in the passenger side.

The detective lit up the car, then tore out of the parking lot. Brenda grabbed the handle of the door to steady herself as he wove through traffic. As she looked over at him, she could see the tension in his face. She realized in that moment that Detective Crackle was just as determined to find Joyce as she was.

The parking lot for *Country Grocery Place* was packed. He drove straight up to the entrance and climbed out of the car. Behind him a few patrol cars pulled up.

"I want this entire store sealed off!" He barked at the officers who ran up to him.

"What should we tell the manager, sir?" The youngest of the group gazed at him.

"You tell him to lock the doors and account for all of his employees. No one goes in or out. Understand?" The detective clapped his hands together. "Now!"

"Yes, sir." The officers took off into the grocery store.

"She could be out here in one of these cars." The detective placed his hands on his hips as he turned to scan the parking lot. "It looks like just about every space is taken."

"She has to be here somewhere." Brenda scanned the faces of the people on the sidewalks that had managed to make it out of the store before the doors were locked. "Detective, if Mark is planning something, then I'd guess he'd want as much attention as possible. My guess is he's inside."

"That's a good guess." Detective Crackle took his hat off and wiped the back of his hand across his forehead.

"So, let's look for her, we might not have much time."

"Okay." Detective Crackle cleared his throat as

he set the hat back on his head. "Let's start inside. I'll have the patrolmen do a sweep of the parking lot."

"I just hope it will be enough." Brenda did her best to keep her stomach calm. "Anything could be happening to her right now, and we don't even know for sure that Mark has her. Maybe Poppy does?" She shook her head. "Maybe Mark forced her into it?"

"Maybe." Detective Crackle led her through the front door of the grocery store. Several people were gathered near the front, and all seemed restless, if not upset.

Brenda looked through all of their faces, and tried to remember if they were familiar. It was nearly impossible as she saw so many people at the donut truck on a daily basis, that just about everyone in town looked familiar. As Detective Crackle got involved with talking to the manager of the store, she wandered off. If whoever had Joyce was there, she doubted they would be hiding among the crowd. She began to walk the aisles of the grocery store. With everyone corralled in the front of the store, the rest of it was eerily empty.

"Joyce?" Brenda stood in the middle of the

frozen section and looked at the coolers. "Joyce! Can you hear me?"

Tears welled up in Brenda's eyes as she received no response. Then she spotted it, a glint of green in the corner near the door that led to the cooler. The sight of it made her head spin both with relief and fear. How much time did she have left to save her? Or was she already too late?

CHAPTER 15

*J*oyce shivered. The cold air of the freezer had begun to sink into her bones. Although she still felt young in spirit, at times she did feel like she was getting older. After a yoga class, and whenever it was very cold. It made her body ache. Her eyes watered as she had yet to take them off Poppy, who paced back and forth near the freezer door. She paused, then peeked out through the door.

"The cops are out there. This wasn't supposed to happen. Why are the cops out there?" Poppy spun on her heel and looked at Joyce. "It's because of you, isn't it? Are they looking for you?"

"I don't know." Joyce shivered again, the cold air sunk deeper into her bones. "Poppy, if you just come clean about all of this now, the police will make a deal with you."

"Nonsense!" Poppy growled at Joyce. "No, this is just fine. It'll make an even bigger statement." She drew a deep breath, then rubbed her hands together. "It's time to make sure that the message is delivered." She looked back at Joyce. "Stand up." She pulled a thick, black marker out of her pocket.

"Why?" Joyce huddled back on the crates in the corner of the freezer.

"Just be still." Poppy approached her. "This can be done the easy way, or the hard way." She uncapped the lid of the marker and held it up in the air.

"Poppy, that's not going to work. No one is going to bother to read the message. Don't you see? They're only going to call you a murderer, they're only going to focus on that. Your message will get lost, because everyone will talk about what a terrible thing you did instead of why you did it." Joyce ducked her head away from the tip of the marker.

"You're wrong! The only way people will listen is if you shock them! That's what I tried to teach Alexa. The people have to be woken up first, they have to be jolted out of their stupor so that they can actually hear the message, and see the truth."

"But they didn't hear you when you dropped Alexa's body at the town square, did they?" Joyce gulped back a sob as Poppy grabbed her arm and began to scrawl across her skin.

"I didn't make the message clear. I will this time. When they find your body sprawled out in the produce section, with the details of how each organ in your body was poisoned by their chemicals, that is something they won't be able to ignore!" Poppy jerked Joyce's arm towards her. "Be still!"

Joyce took a deep breath. She knew that her only option for escape was to overpower Poppy. But Poppy was much stronger than she was, and fixated on making sure that Joyce became her palette.

"Why don't you just let me say all of those things? Poppy, you could walk out there with me right now. Show me to the police. Demand a news camera. You could say everything you have to say, and people will be shocked." Joyce closed her eyes tight as the marker dug into her arm. "Please."

"Why, so they can kill me? So I can spend the rest of my life in prison?" Poppy shook her head. "No, I will be walking out of here before they have a chance to catch me."

As she spoke, the freezer door swung open.

"Poppy?" Mark's voice carried through the freezer. "Poppy, are you in here?"

Poppy froze. She looked over her shoulder as Mark approached with a pile of signs in his hands.

"Go away, Mark. I am handling this myself, now."

"Why? I brought the signs. You agreed not to wait, we were going to do this—" His voice cut off as he caught sight of Joyce. "What is going on here?"

"She's going to kill me, Mark!" Joyce had no idea whether he was involved or not, but she was desperate, and he was her only chance. "Please! Help me!"

"Kill you?" Mark dropped the signs that he held. "Poppy! What is she talking about? We were just supposed to hang some signs."

"Signs! Really, Mark? Do you think that's going to change anything? No, it's not. You and Alexa were both too scared to do what needed to be done. But I'm not, I'm not scared at all! Like I told you when I tried to stop you from instigating the violence at the protest. A punch isn't going to make a difference, it's going to distract from the real message. You need to take drastic action to make a change, but you never listened to me!"

"Poppy, what have you done?" Mark reached for her, just as Poppy pulled a gun out of her purse and aimed it at him.

"Don't! Don't take a single step closer to me. I will not let anyone stop me! I came here to send a message, and I'm going to send it, no matter what it takes. You can either help me send the message, Mark, or you can be part of it. Which would you prefer?"

"Poppy, you don't have to do this. We can get the audience to hear us. I will get our message across on the videos. I've already deleted some of Alexa's videos, so we can take the limelight. Please stop, Poppy," Mark pleaded. "You don't have to do this."

Joyce knew that she only had one chance. She eased up off the crates she had been sitting on and grabbed one. As she swung it through the air, she was aware that the moment she made impact, that gun would likely swing towards her. Despite her petite size she put all of the force she could muster into that swing, and cracked the crate down over the top of Poppy's head.

As she did, a gunshot rang out. In the confined space, the gunshot sounded so loud that it made Joyce's head spin. Pain flashed through her body.

Had she been shot? Had Poppy anticipated her attack and swung around before she had the chance to strike?

Poppy slumped down to her knees. Across from her, so did Mark. He grabbed at his stomach and let out a low groan. Joyce tried to make sense of the situation. But she didn't have long to try to figure it out. Because Poppy jumped right back up to her feet, and spun around to face her.

"You shouldn't have done that. You threw off my aim. Now Mark is going to suffer because I couldn't get a clean shot to his head. What kind of monster are you?" Poppy pointed the gun directly in her face. "You're just like the rest of them, selfish! You'd rather protect yourself than wake up your own community. You disgust me."

"I'm sorry, Poppy, let's get Mark some help, please!" Joyce gasped as Mark continued to clutch at his stomach.

"I am helping him! And I'm helping you! Now be still, I can do this with you alive or after you're dead." Poppy pulled out her marker again.

Joyce froze. She hoped that whatever message Poppy wanted to write would take her some time. Long enough for someone to save her.

Brenda jumped and gasped at the sound of the gunshot. She grabbed Detective Crackle's arm.

He pushed her away as he drew his own weapon, then nudged the freezer door open.

Brenda could see his muscles strain as he attempted to resist barging in. "Stay here!" He shot her a look of warning.

Brenda held her breath as he stepped through the doors. The last thing she intended to do was stay there. She had to find out what was happening in that freezer. She ran along the freezer doors. She could catch glimpses of the areas inside the freezer through the shelving that displayed the frozen foods. But she couldn't see enough to spot Joyce.

A flood of police officers headed towards the freezer, summoned by the sound of the gunshot. Brenda watched as they surrounded the area. But something didn't sit right with her. Why would a murderer go into an area that couldn't be escaped? She was quite certain that wouldn't happen. Her heart pounded as she realized there had to be another exit. With most of the police presence inside the store, the murderer just might escape while they looked in the freezer.

CINDY BELL

Brenda tried to escape through the nearest exit door, but when she slammed her hands into it, she found it was locked. She ran towards the front of the store, determined to get out. As she neared the front doors, an officer stepped in front of her.

"No one can leave!"

"Open that door or I will break it open!" Brenda swung her foot back to kick it.

The officer lunged for her before she could.

"Stop!" Detective Crackle ran up between them. "It's okay, she's with me."

"Are you sure?" The officer frowned as he eyed her with some confusion. "She was about to kick through the door."

"I'm sure. Brenda, what are you doing?" Detective Crackle turned to face her.

"She wasn't in there, was she?" She stared at him, her cheeks flushed as her heart pounded. "Joyce?"

"No, she wasn't. Mark was." He tipped his head towards a gurney that was being wheeled towards the door. "He's been shot, he's unconscious, but he should be fine. Joyce must have gotten the gun from him."

"No!" Brenda's head spun. "No, she wouldn't

have shot him and then run. No, someone else has her! We need to get to the parking lot before they get away." She stepped aside as the gurney rolled past them. "If it's not Mark, then maybe it's Poppy!" She bolted through the door and out into the parking lot. She saw the ambulance, and several police cars. Then she caught sight of a car nearing the exit of the parking lot. "That's it!" She shouted as she broke into a run. "That's the car! It has no taillights!"

Detective Crackle barked into his radio as he chased after Brenda.

"We'll never catch them on foot, Brenda." He pulled his gun and aimed for the car.

"No don't!" Brenda shrieked. "What if she's in the trunk? What if you hit her?"

"You have to trust me, Brenda." Detective Crackle stared into her eyes briefly, then aimed his weapon.

Brenda's stomach lurched as he fired twice. She continued to run towards the car, which veered off to the right.

Detective Crackle had managed to strike both back tires. He ran a few steps behind her towards the car. The driver's side door flung open, and Poppy tumbled out. She jumped to her feet and sprinted for the neighborhood that bordered the parking lot.

"Stop!" Detective Crackle shouted. "Get on your knees!"

Poppy spun around to face both of them. She let out a loud laugh that sounded more like a spasm than an actual laugh. Brenda ignored her as she ran straight for the car. She had no idea if Joyce was in the car, or if she was even still alive. But she knew that she had to find out. As she reached the car, she found the passenger seat was empty. Her heart dropped at the sight. Then she heard a noise from the backseat. She peered into it and saw Joyce curled up on the floor. She had a piece of tape over her mouth and her hands were bound as well.

"Joyce!" Brenda pulled open the back door and crouched down to free her hands. "Are you hurt? Did she hurt you?"

Joyce shook her head, and as soon as her hands were free she pulled the tape off her mouth with a subtle shout.

"Oh Brenda, I'm so glad to see you." She threw her arms around her waist and rested her head against her stomach. "Please, just let me hug you for a minute."

"Joyce, I'm so sorry." She stroked her hair as

she held her close. "I never should have let you go off on your own. I let you walk into danger!"

"No, you didn't." Joyce looked up at her. "I did what I wanted to do, I put myself in that danger. I never realized that it was Poppy, I didn't think it would be her. I let her fool me. Mark had no idea what she was doing."

"It's okay now, that's all that matters. You're safe." Brenda felt her muscles relax some as she caught sight of Detective Crackle arresting Poppy. "I was so scared."

"So was I." Joyce shuddered. "I have to admit that might have been too much adventure for me."

Brenda helped her out of the car and looked her over from head to toe. "Are you sure you're okay? She didn't hurt you?"

"No, she didn't. But she did kill Alexa, and she tried to kill Mark." She held out her arms to reveal the writing scrawled across them. "She was more concerned with getting her message across than killing me."

"I'm so sorry you went through that, Joyce."

After Detective Crackle handed Poppy off to other officers, he walked over to them.

"Joyce." He stared into her eyes. "The paramedics are waiting to look you over."

"There's no need, I'm fine. Just let me give you my statement so I can go." Joyce ran her hands across her cheeks. "Honestly, I can't wait to get back to the truck. I just want things to go back to normal as soon as possible."

"I understand." The detective reached up and tucked some of her hair back behind her ear. "I'm sorry it took us so long to find you."

"You saved me." Joyce caught his hand and held it with her own. "Thank you, Detective."

"Don't forget it's Arthur. Call me Arthur, if you like."

"Thank you, I haven't forgotten." Joyce gave his hand a light squeeze.

After they gave their statements, Brenda called Melissa. She knew that if she called Charlie to come get her, he would have to bring Sophie with him, and she wouldn't want to try to explain things in front of her. It was almost closing time so she asked Melissa to close down the truck and pick them up from the grocery store. As they waited for her to arrive, Joyce filled Brenda in on all that Poppy told her.

"I can't believe that she killed her best friend, all over her beliefs." Brenda shook her head. "Don't worry, Joyce, I could never do that to you."

"Gee, thanks." Joyce managed a smile.

When Melissa pulled up, she jumped out of the car and ran to embrace both of them.

"I heard what happened, are you both okay?" Melissa looked between them. Then she looked tentatively at the huddle of police officers.

"We're okay." Brenda eyed her. "Now Melissa, why don't you tell me why you are so afraid of the police?"

"I'm not afraid, exactly." Melissa shifted from one foot to the other. "The truth is, this is all my fault."

"What do you mean?" Joyce studied her.

"I mean, I sent a message to Alexa suggesting that she come to the magazine event. I never thought she would. But maybe if I hadn't sent that email, maybe she never would have come here and then—"

"Oh, sweetheart." Brenda hugged her and shook her head. "None of this is your fault. She probably got thousands of emails. She came here because *Country Grocery Place* was opening here, not because you told her to come. I'm sorry you've been feeling that way all this time. You should have told me."

"You're right." Melissa wiped her eyes as she pulled out of the hug. "It's just that I enjoy working with you both so much, I didn't want to do anything to risk that."

"There is no risk, Melissa. We are happy to have you." Brenda smiled at her.

"Yes, it's good to know I'm not the only one that can burn donuts." Joyce laughed.

"Oh, you mean today wasn't the first time?" Brenda raised her eyebrows.

"You promised you wouldn't tell, Joyce." Melissa blushed.

"Oh, it's okay." Brenda laughed. "Did I ever tell you two about the time I started a fire in the kitchen?"

The three walked off towards Melissa's car, laughing, despite the ordeal they just endured. Brenda slipped her hand into Joyce's and held it tight. It would be a long time before she would be willing to let it go.

The End

ALSO BY CINDY BELL

DONUT TRUCK COZY MYSTERIES

Deadly Deals and Donuts

Fatal Festive Donuts

Bunny Donuts and a Body

SAGE GARDENS COZY MYSTERIES

Birthdays Can Be Deadly

Money Can Be Deadly

Trust Can Be Deadly

Ties Can Be Deadly

Rocks Can Be Deadly

Jewelry Can Be Deadly

Numbers Can Be Deadly

Memories Can Be Deadly

Paintings Can Be Deadly

Snow Can Be Deadly

Tea Can Be Deadly

Greed Can Be Deadly

Clutter Can Be Deadly

WAGGING TAIL COZY MYSTERIES

Murder at Pooch Park

Murder at the Pet Boutique

CHOCOLATE CENTERED COZY MYSTERIES

The Sweet Smell of Murder

A Deadly Delicious Delivery

A Bitter Sweet Murder

A Treacherous Tasty Trail

Pastry and Peril

Trouble and Treats

Fudge Films and Felonies

Custom-Made Murder

Skydiving, Soufflés and Sabotage

Christmas Chocolates and Crimes

Hot Chocolate and Homicide

Chocolate Caramels and Conmen

Picnics, Pies and Lies

DUNE HOUSE COZY MYSTERIES

Seaside Secrets

Boats and Bad Guys

Treasured History

Hidden Hideaways

Dodgy Dealings

Suspects and Surprises

Ruffled Feathers

A Fishy Discovery

Danger in the Depths

Celebrities and Chaos

Pups, Pilots and Peril

Tides, Trails and Trouble

Racing and Robberies

Athletes and Alibis

BEKKI THE BEAUTICIAN COZY MYSTERIES

Hairspray and Homicide

A Dyed Blonde and a Dead Body

Mascara and Murder

Pageant and Poison

Conditioner and a Corpse

Mistletoe, Makeup and Murder

Hairpin, Hair Dryer and Homicide

Blush, a Bride and a Body

Shampoo and a Stiff

Cosmetics, a Cruise and a Killer

Lipstick, a Long Iron and Lifeless

Camping, Concealer and Criminals

Treated and Dyed

A Wrinkle-Free Murder

A MACARON PATISSERIE COZY MYSTERY SERIES

Sifting for Suspects

Recipes and Revenge

Mansions, Macarons and Murder

NUTS ABOUT NUTS COZY MYSTERIES

A Tough Case to Crack

A Seed of Doubt

Roasted Penuts and Peril

HEAVENLY HIGHLAND INN COZY MYSTERIES

Murdering the Roses

Dead in the Daisies

Killing the Carnations

Drowning the Daffodils

Suffocating the Sunflowers

Books, Bullets and Blooms

A Deadly Serious Gardening Contest

A Bridal Bouquet and a Body

Digging for Dirt

WENDY THE WEDDING PLANNER COZY MYSTERIES

Matrimony, Money and Murder

Chefs, Ceremonies and Crimes

Knives and Nuptials

Mice, Marriage and Murder

ABOUT THE AUTHOR

Cindy Bell is a USA Today and Wall Street Journal Bestselling Author. She is the author of the cozy mystery series Wagging Tail, Donut Truck, Dune House, Sage Gardens, Chocolate Centered, Macaron Patisserie, Nuts about Nuts, Bekki the Beautician, Heavenly Highland Inn and Wendy the Wedding Planner.

Cindy has always loved reading, but it is only recently that she has discovered her passion for writing romantic cozy mysteries. She loves walking along the beach thinking of the next adventure her characters can embark on.

You can sign up for her newsletter so you are notified of her latest releases at http://www.cindybellbooks.com.

BAKED STRAWBERRY DONUTS

Ingredients:

Donuts

1/2 cup butter
1 1/4 cups all-purpose flour
1 teaspoon baking powder
1/2 teaspoon baking soda
1/2 cup superfine sugar
1 egg
1 teaspoon vanilla extract
1/2 cup Greek yogurt
1/4 cup finely chopped strawberries

Strawberry Glaze

BAKED STRAWBERRY DONUTS

2 cups confectioners' sugar
1 cup diced strawberries

Sprinkles for decorating (optional)

Preparation:

Makes 10 donuts.

Preheat the oven to 350 degrees Fahrenheit. Grease a donut pan.

Melt the butter and set aside to cool.

Sieve the flour, baking powder and baking soda into a bowl.

Add the superfine sugar and mix together.

In another bowl mix together the melted butter, egg and vanilla extract.

Gradually add the egg mixture alternating with the yogurt, to the dry ingredients. Stir until just combined.

BAKED STRAWBERRY DONUTS

Fold in the chopped strawberries.

Spoon the mixture into the prepared donut pan.

Bake for 8-10 minutes. The donuts are ready when a skewer inserted into the middle comes out clean.

To prepare the glaze heat the strawberries for about 10 minutes in a pan over medium heat, stirring occasionally. The mixture should be the consistency of a thick sauce. It is okay to still have some strawberry pieces in the sauce. Cool slightly and puree in a food processor to a smooth consistency.

Gradually whisk the confectioners' sugar into the strawberry mixture until the mixture is at the desired consistency and color.

Dip the donuts in the glaze to cover the tops completely. Decorate with sprinkles if desired. Leave at room temperature to set.

Enjoy!!

CPSIA information can be obtained
at www.ICGtesting.com
Printed in the USA
LVHW081832170120
644014LV00033B/1304